THE LAND OF
GREEN PLUMS

THE LAND OF GREEN PLUMS

a novel

Herta Müller

Translated by Michael Hofmann

METROPOLITAN BOOKS
Henry Holt and Company
New York

Metropolitan Books
Henry Holt and Company, Inc.
Publishers since 1866
115 West 18th Street
New York, New York 10011

Metropolitan Books™ is an imprint of Henry Holt and Company, Inc.
Copyright © 1993 by Rowohlt Verlag GMBH
English translation copyright © 1996 by Metropolitan Books
All rights reserved.

Originally published in Germany in 1993
under the title *Herztier* by Rowohlt Verlag.

Library of Congress Cataloging-in-Publication Data
Müller, Herta.
[Herztier. English]
The land of green plums : a novel / Herta Müller : translated by
Michael Hofmann. — 1st American ed.
p.   cm.
I. Hofmann, Michael.   II. Title.
PT2673.U29234H4713   1996   96-7305
833'.914—dc20   CIP
ISBN 0-8050-4295-4

Henry Holt books are available for special
promotions and premiums. For details contact:
Director, Special Markets.

First American Edition—1996

Designed by Paula R. Szafranski

Printed in the United States of America
All first editions are printed on acid-free paper. ∞

3   5   7   9   10   8   6   4   2

The publisher wishes to thank Philip Boehm
for his help in preparing this edition.

Everyone had a friend in every wisp of cloud
that's how it is with friends where the world is full of fear
even my mother said, that's how it is
friends are out of the question
think of more serious things.

Gellu Naum

THE LAND OF
GREEN PLUMS

When we don't speak, said Edgar, we become unbearable, and when we do, we make fools of ourselves.

We had been sitting and staring at the pictures on the floor for too long. My legs had fallen asleep from sitting.

The words in our mouths do as much damage as our feet on the grass. But so do our silences.

Edgar was silent.

To this day, I can't really picture a grave. Only a belt, a window, a nut, and a rope. To me, each death is like a sack.

Anyone who hears that, said Edgar, is bound to think you've lost your mind.

And then, I have the feeling that whenever someone dies he leaves behind a sack of words. And barbers, and nail-clippers—I always think of them, too, since the dead

1

no longer need them. And they don't ever lose buttons either.

Maybe they sensed the dictator was a mistake in a different way than we did, said Edgar.

They had proof enough, because even we considered ourselves a mistake. Because in this country, we had to walk, eat, sleep, and love in fear, until it was once again time for the barber and the nail-clippers.

Anyone who makes graveyards just because he walks, eats, sleeps, and loves, said Edgar, is a bigger mistake than we are. A mistake of the first order. A master mistake.

The grass stands tall inside our heads. When we speak it gets mowed. Even when we don't. And then the second, and the third growth springs up at will. And even so: We are the lucky ones.

Lola came from the south of the country, and she reeked of poor province. I don't know where it showed the most, maybe in her cheekbones, or around her mouth, or smack in the middle of her eyes. It's hard to say that sort of thing about a province or a face. There was poverty in every province in the country, and in every face. But Lola's province, whether you saw it in her cheekbones or around her mouth or smack in the middle of her eyes, was perhaps poorer still. More land than landscape.

The drought devours everything, Lola writes, except sheep, melons, and mulberry trees.

But it wasn't the dry province that drove Lola to the city.

The drought couldn't care less about what I'm learning, Lola writes in her notebook. The drought doesn't realize how much I know. Only what I am, or really who. To become somebody in the city, writes Lola, and then, four years later, to go back to the village. Not on the dusty path down below, but higher up, through the branches of the mulberry trees.

There were mulberry trees in the city as well. But not on the streets outside. In courtyards. And not in many. Only in old peoples' courtyards. And under the trees stood a house chair. The seat was upholstered with velvet. But the velvet was stained and torn. And the hole had been plugged from beneath with a bunch of hay. The hay was flattened from being sat on. It dangled from the chair like a pigtail.

If you went up to the discarded chair, you could make out the individual strands of hay. And that they had once been green.

Inside the mulberry courtyards, shade fell like calm on an old face sitting in the chair. Like calm, because I ventured into these courtyards unexpectedly, even to myself, and only rarely revisited them. On those rare occasions, a ray of light fell straight from the treetop onto the old face and revealed a faraway province. I looked up and down this ray. I felt a shiver run down my spine, because the calm didn't come from the mulberry branches; it came from the loneliness of the eyes in the face. I didn't want anyone to see me in those courtyards. Anyone to ask me what I was doing here. I wasn't doing anything, I was just there. I stared at the mulberry trees for a long time. And then, before I left, one last look at the face sitting on the chair. There was a province in the face. I saw a young man or a young woman leaving the province, carrying a sack, a sack with a mulberry tree in it. I saw every mulberry tree that had been carried into the courtyards of the city.

Later I read in Lola's notebook: Whatever you carry out of your province, you carry into your face.

Lola wanted to spend four years studying Russian. The entrance exam had been easy, because there were enough places at the university, as many as there were schools in the country. And Russian wasn't high on many people's list of wishes. Wishes are difficult, writes Lola, goals are easier. A man who studies something, writes Lola, has clean fingernails. In four years he'll come back with me, because a man like that knows he'll be respected in the village. He knows the barber will call on him at his house, and leave his shoes at the door. No more sheep, writes Lola, no more melons, only mulberry trees, because all of us have leaves.

A little cube of a room, one window, six girls, six beds, under each a suitcase. Next to the door, a closet built into the wall; in the ceiling over the door, a loudspeaker. The workers' choruses sang from the ceiling to the wall, from the wall to the beds, until night fell. Then they grew quiet, like the street below the window and the scruffy park, which no one walked through anymore. There were forty identical little cubes in each dormitory.

Someone said, The loudspeakers see and hear everything we do.

The dresses of the six girls hung tightly pressed together in the closet. Lola had fewer than anyone else. She wore all of theirs. The girls' stockings lay inside the suitcases under the beds.

Someone sang:

If ever I marry,
so Mama says
this gift she'll give me
on my wedding day:
twenty big pillows
all stuffed with biting gnats,
twenty small pillows,
all stuffed with stinging ants,
twenty soft pillows
all stuffed with rotten leaves

and Lola sat on the floor beside her bed and opened her suitcase. She rummaged through her stockings and held up a tangle of legs and toes and heels in front of her face. She let the stockings drop to the floor. Her hands were shaking, and she had more eyes than the two in her face. Her hands were empty, and she had more hands than the two in the air. There were almost as many hands in the air as there were stockings on the floor.

So many eyes, hands, and stockings couldn't possibly fit inside one song, sung across two narrow beds. Sung while standing, by a little head that swayed, with a furrow in its brow. A song from which the furrow immediately disappeared.

Under each bed lay a suitcase full of jumbled cotton stockings. They were called patent stockings all over the country. Heavy stockings for girls who wanted nylon hose, smooth and whisper-thin. And hairspray, and mascara, and nail polish.

Under the pillows in the beds were six pots of mascara. Six girls spat into the pots and stirred the soot with toothpicks until the black paste grew sticky. Then they opened their eyes wide. The toothpicks scraped against their eyelids, their lashes grew black and thick. But an hour later gray gaps began to crack open in the eyelashes. The saliva dried up and the soot crumbled onto their cheeks.

The girls wanted soot on their cheeks, as long as it was mascara soot, but never again the soot of factories. Just plenty of whisper-thin nylons, since they ran so easily, and the girls had to catch the runs at the ankles and thighs. Catch them and patch them with nail polish.

It will be hard to keep the shirts of a gentleman white. If, in four years, he comes back with me to the drought, it will be because of my love. If his white shirts manage to dazzle the people walking in the village, it will be because of my love. And it will be my love if he proves a gentleman, on whom the barber will call at home, leaving his shoes at the door. It will be difficult to keep the shirts white with all that dirt and all those leaping fleas, writes Lola.

Lola said, Fleas even on the bark of trees. Someone said, Those aren't fleas. They're lice, leaf-lice. Lola writes in her notebook: Leaf-fleas are even worse. Someone said, They don't bite people, because people don't have leaves. Lola writes, When the sun is beating down, they bite everything, even the wind. And we all have leaves. Leaves fall off when you stop growing, because childhood is all gone. And they grow back when you shrivel up, because love is all gone. Leaves spring up at will, writes Lola, just like tall grass. Two or three children in the village don't have any leaves, and those have a big childhood. A child like that is an only child, because it has a father and a mother who have been to school. The leaf-fleas turn older children into younger ones—a four-year-old into a three-year-old, a three-year-old into a one-year-old. Even a six-month-old, writes Lola, and even a newborn. And the more little brothers and sisters the leaf-fleas make, the smaller the childhood becomes.

A grandfather says: My pruning shears. I'm getting older and shorter and thinner with every passing day. But my nails are growing faster and thicker. He uses the pruning shears to cut his nails.

A child refuses to let her nails be cut. That hurts, says the child. The mother ties the child to a chair with the belts from her dresses. The child's eyes cloud over, and she starts

7

to scream. The mother keeps dropping the nail-clippers onto the floor. One fall for each finger, the child thinks.

Blood drips onto one of the belts, the grass-green one. The child knows, if you bleed, you die. The child's eyes are wet; they see the mother through a blur. The mother loves the child. She loves it like crazy, and she can't stop herself, because her reason is as tightly tied to love as her child is to the chair. The child knows: the mother in her tightly tied love is going to cut up her hands. Then she'll have to stick the cut-off fingers in the pocket of her housedress and go into the courtyard, as if she meant to throw them away. And in the yard, where no one can see her, she'll have to eat the child's fingers.

The child suspects that the mother is going to lie and nod her head when the grandfather asks her that evening: Did you throw the fingers away?

And the child suspects what she is going to do that evening as well. *She took the fingers,* she will say, and describe everything:

Mother went out on the pavement with the fingers. She was on the grass. She was in the garden as well, on the path and in the flowerbeds. She walked next to the wall and went behind the wall too. She was at the tool cupboard with the screws. She was at the wardrobe. She opened the door and cried. She wiped her cheek with one hand, and kept taking the other hand out of the pocket of her housedress and sticking it in her mouth. Again and again.

The grandfather puts his hand over his mouth. Maybe he wants to show, right here in this room, how fingers are eaten out in the yard, the child thinks. But the grandfather's hand doesn't move.

The child goes on talking. As she speaks, something gets stuck on her tongue. The child thinks, it can only be the truth sticking to her tongue like a cherrystone that refuses to go down her throat. As long as her voice keeps rising to her ears, she will wait for the truth. But once her voice grows silent, thinks the child, everything will turn out to have been a lie, since the truth has gone tumbling down her throat. Because her mouth failed to say the words *and ate them*.

The child can't get the words past her lips. Only:

She had been to the plum tree. She wasn't the one who stepped on the caterpillar in the garden path, her shoe just missed it.

The grandfather lowers his eyes.

Now the mother creates a distraction by fetching a needle and thread from the cupboard. She sits on the chair and smoothes out her housedress until you can see the pocket. She knots the thread. Mother is stitching a lie, the child thinks.

The mother sews on a button. The new thread covers the old. There is some truth in the mother's lie, because the button on her housedress is loose. The button gets the thickest thread. The electric light bulb is thready like that, too.

Then the child squeezes her eyes shut. Behind her closed eyes, Mother and Grandfather are hanging over the table from a rope of thread and light.

The button with the thickest thread will last the longest. Mother will never lose it, thinks the child, it will break first.

The mother tosses the clippers back into the linen cupboard. The next day and every Wednesday after that, the grandfather's barber will come into the room.

My barber, says the grandfather.

My scissors, says the barber.

In the First World War all my hair fell out, says the grandfather. When my head was quite bald, the company barber rubbed some leaf extract into my scalp. My hair grew back. Better than ever, the company barber told me. He liked to play chess. He got the idea for the leaf extract because I had brought along some leafy branches from which I was carving a chess set. There were red leaves and ash-gray leaves on different branches of the same tree. And the wood was just as varied as the leaves. I carved a dark and a light set of chessmen. The light leaves didn't turn dark until late autumn. The trees had these two colors because every year the ash-gray branches took a long time before sprouting. The two colors were good for my chess set, said the grandfather.

First the barber cuts the grandfather's hair. The grandfather sits on the chair without moving his head. The barber says: If you don't cut your hair, your head will grow into a scruffy thicket. Meanwhile, the mother ties the child to the chair with the belts. The barber says: If you don't cut your nails, your fingers will grow into shovels. Only the dead are allowed to do that.

Untie me, untie me.

Of the six girls in the cube, Lola had the fewest whisper-thin nylons. And those few were patched together with nail polish at the ankles and thighs, and at the calves as well. They kept running, too, and Lola couldn't catch them, because she had to keep running herself, up and down the sidewalk or through the scruffy park.

With her desire for white shirts, Lola had to keep running off and running after. Even at the best of times, her desire remained as poor as the province in her face.

At times Lola couldn't catch her running nylons because she was attending the meeting. At the department head's house, said Lola, not realizing how much she liked that title, department head.

At night Lola hung her nylons out the window feet first. They couldn't drip because they were never washed. They hung from the window as though Lola's feet and legs were in them, her toes and her hard heels, her swollen calves and knees. They could have walked through the scruffy park and into the dark city even without Lola.

Someone in the little cube asked, Where are my nail-clippers? Lola said, In the coat pocket. Someone asked, In whose? In yours? How is it you went off with them again yesterday? I was in the tram, Lola said, laying the nail-clippers on the bed.

Lola always cut her nails on the tram. Often she would just ride around aimlessly. She would cut and file away in the moving vehicle, pushing the cuticle back with her teeth until the white oval on each nail was the size of a little bean.

At the stops, Lola would slip the nail-clippers in her pocket and watch the door to see whether anyone got on. Because during the day some man is always getting on as if he knows me already, writes Lola in her notebook, but during the night the same man gets on as though he is looking for me.

At night, when there was no longer anyone passing through the scruffy park, you could hear the wind, and its sound was all there was left of the sky. Then Lola would put on her whisper-thin nylons. And before she shut the door from the outside, in the light of the cube you could see that Lola had a second pair of feet. Someone asked, Where are you going? But Lola's footsteps were already clattering down the long, empty corridor.

Maybe, in those first three years in the little room, I was that someone. Because, except for Lola, anyone could have been that someone. And someone in the bright cube did not like Lola. That meant everyone.

Someone went over to the window and saw no street below and no Lola walking down it. Just a tiny skipping dot.

Lola walked to the tram. When someone got on at the next stop, she opened her eyes wide.

Only men got on at midnight, on their way home from the late shift at the detergent factory or the slaughterhouse. They climb out of the night into the light of the streetcar, writes Lola, and I see a man so tired from his day that he's nothing more than a shadow in clothes. There hasn't been any thought of love in his head for a long time, and no money in his leather bag. Only some stolen detergent or hunks of organ meat: beef tongues, pig's kidneys, or a calf's liver.

Lola's men took the first empty seat. They nodded off in the bright light, let their heads droop and jerk to the squealing of the rails. Sooner or later they clutch their bags close to themselves, Lola writes, and I see their dirty hands. Because of their bags, they take a quick look at my face.

In that quick look, Lola would light a fire in a tired head. They don't shut their eyes after that, writes Lola.

One stop later, a man would follow Lola out. In his eyes he carried the darkness of the city. And the greedy desire of a starved dog, writes Lola. She didn't turn around, she walked fast. Leaving the street, she lured the men along the shortest way into the scruffy park. Without a word, writes Lola, I lie down in the grass, and he puts his bag under the longest, lowest branch. There's no need to talk.

The wind chased the night, and Lola tossed her head silently to and fro, and her belly. Leaves rustled across her face, as they had years before over a six-month-old baby, a sixth child wanted by no one but poverty, and just as then, Lola's legs were scratched by the twigs. But never her face.

for months Lola had been changing the newspaper in the glass display case of the dormitory once a week. She stood by the door to the glass case and swayed her hips. She blew away the dead flies and polished the glass with two patent stockings from her suitcase. With one stocking she wet the glass, with the other she rubbed it dry. Then she switched the newspaper clippings, crumpled up the dictator's previous speech, and tacked up the latest one in its place. When Lola was done, she threw the stockings away.

Once Lola had used up almost all the patent stockings in her suitcase, she took stockings from the other suitcases. Someone said, Those aren't yours. Lola said, You wouldn't want to wear them again anyway.

. . .

A father hacks away at the summer in his garden. A child stands next to the garden bed and thinks: Father knows something about life. Because Father stashes his guilty conscience inside the damn stupid plants and hacks them down. A second ago, the child was wishing that the stupid plants could flee the hoe and live out the summer. But they can't flee, because they don't grow their white feathers until autumn. Only then do they learn to fly.

Father never had to flee. He had gone marching off into the world with a song on his lips. In that world he had made graveyards and quickly left them behind. A lost war, an SS-man who came back from the war, a freshly ironed short-sleeved shirt in the wardrobe, and still no gray hairs growing on his head.

Father got up very early. He liked to lie in the grass. As he lay, he would look up at the reddish clouds that brought the day. And because the morning was still as cold as the night, the reddish clouds had to tear up the sky. Daybreak came high above the clouds, while down below in the grass, loneliness came into Father's head. It swiftly drove Father to the warm skin of a woman. He warmed himself. He had made graveyards, and now he quickly made the woman a baby.

Father keeps the graveyards deep in his throat, between his collar and his chin, near his Adam's apple. His Adam's apple sticks out and is locked up. That way the graveyards can never pass his lips. His mouth drinks schnapps made

14

from the darkest plums, and his songs for the Führer are heavy and drunken.

The hoe in the garden bed casts a shadow, which hacks nothing. The shadow keeps still and watches the garden path. It sees a child filling her pockets with green plums.

Standing among the hacked-down, stupid plants, Father says: You can't eat green plums, their pits are still soft, and you'll swallow your death. No one can help then—you just die. The raging fever will burn your heart up from the inside.

The father's eyes swim, and the child can see her father loves her like crazy. That he can't stop himself. That he, who has made graveyards, the child wishes death on.

That's why the child later eats up all the plums in her pockets. Every day when the father isn't watching the child, she stows away whole branches inside her belly. The child eats and thinks, This will kill me.

But the father doesn't see this, and the child doesn't have to die.

The damn stupid plants were milk thistles. Father did know something about life. Just as all the people who talk about death know life really goes on.

Sometimes I saw Lola standing in the shower room in the afternoon, when it was too late to wash for the day and too early for the night. I saw a scabby rope down Lola's back and a scabby circle over her buttocks. The rope and the circle made a shape like a pendulum.

Lola quickly turned away, and I saw the pendulum reflected in the mirror. It must have struck the hour, because Lola jumped when I came into the shower room.

I thought: Lola wears their scratches, but never their love. Only thrusts into her belly on the ground in the park. And above her the doggish eyes of men who hear detergent falling down a thick tube all day long, and the death rattle of beasts. At night, those eyes glowed and burned over Lola, because they had been extinguished throughout the day.

On every floor of the dormitory, all the girls inside the cubes shared a small eating area and a common fridge. Sheep's cheese and sausage from home, eggs and mustard.

When I opened the fridge I would find a tongue or a kidney in the farthest corner all the way at the back of the compartment. The tongue would be dried out from the cold, the kidney brown and split. Three days later, the space at the back was empty once again.

I saw the poor province in Lola's face. Whether she ate the tongue and the kidneys or threw them away, I could never tell, neither in her cheekbones, nor around her mouth, nor smack in the middle of her eyes.

Neither in the cafeteria nor in the gym hall could I tell whether Lola ate the bits of organ meat or whether she threw them away. I wanted to know. My curiosity burned to hurt Lola. I watched until my eyes gave out. But whether I stared at Lola or just glanced in her direction, all I ever saw was the province in her face. I only caught Lola frying eggs on the hot iron, scraping them off with a knife and eating them.

Lola offered me a bladeful to taste. It's good, said Lola, not greasy like it is from the pan. Once Lola had eaten, she put the iron away in a corner.

Someone said: Clean the iron after you've eaten. And Lola said: It's no good for ironing anymore anyway.

This blindness tormented me. When I lined up with Lola in the cafeteria for the midday meal and afterward sat at a table with her, I thought: This blindness comes from having been given only spoons to eat with. Never a knife, never a fork. From having to use our spoons to saw away at the meat on our plates and then pull at it with our teeth and tear off little bites. Our blindness, I thought, comes from never being allowed to cut with a knife or spear with a fork. From having to eat like beasts.

In the cafeteria everyone is hungry, writes Lola in her notebook, the whole chomping, lipsmacking lot. By themselves, each one is a stubborn sheep. Taken together, they're a pack of famished dogs.

In the gym I thought, I have this blindness because Lola can't vault over the horse, because she bends her elbows instead of keeping them stiff, because she draws her knees up to her belly instead of parting her legs like scissor blades. Lola got stuck and slid over the horse on her behind. She never sailed over it. She landed on the mat on her face, not on her feet. She stayed lying on the mat till the instructor yelled at her.

Lola knew the gym instructor would pull her up by her

shoulders, her hips, her behind. That once his rage was over he would touch her anywhere at all. Lola made herself heavy, so that he would have to hold on to her more tightly.

All the girls had to stay waiting on the other side of the horse; no one could vault and no one could soar, because Lola was getting a glass of cold water from the gym instructor. He brought it from the changing room and held it to her lips. Lola knew he would hold her head longer if she took her time drinking the water.

After gym the girls stood in front of the narrow lockers in the changing room and put their clothes back on. Someone said, That's my blouse you're wearing. Lola said, I'm not going to eat it, I only need it for today, I've got something planned.

Every day someone in the little cube would say: Those clothes, you know, don't belong to you. But Lola put them on and went out into the city. Day after day she put on the clothes. They were wrinkled and damp with sweat or from rain and snow. Afterward Lola stuffed them back inside the closet.

There were fleas in the closet, because there were fleas in the beds, in the suitcases with the patent stockings, in the long corridor. And in the eating area as well, and in the shower room, and in the cafeteria, there were fleas. In the trams, in the shops, in the movie theater.

Everyone has to scratch as they pray, Lola writes in her notebook. She went to church every Sunday morning. The priest has to scratch himself as well. Our Father, Who art in Heaven, writes Lola; here the whole city is alive with fleas.

. . .

It was evening in the little cube, but not yet late. The loud-speaker was chanting its proletarian songs, shoes were still walking up and down the street outside; there were still voices in the scruffy park, the leaves were still gray and not yet black.

Lola lay on her bed, wearing her thick stockings and nothing else. My brother drives the sheep home in the evening, writes Lola. He has to cross through a melon field. He's left the pasture too late, it's getting dark, and the sheep with their bony shanks are stepping on the melons and smashing them. My brother sleeps in the shed, and the sheep have red feet the whole night long.

Lola pushed an empty bottle between her legs, she tossed her head to and fro, and her belly. All the girls were standing around her bed. Someone pulled her hair. Someone laughed out loud. Someone put her hand to her mouth and stared. Someone began to cry. I no longer remember which of them was me.

But I remember how dizzy I felt that evening, looking out the window for a long time. The room was swinging in the windowpane. I saw all of us, looking very small, standing around Lola's bed. And above and beyond our heads I saw Lola, looking very large, as she stepped through the air and out the closed window into the scruffy park. I saw Lola's men standing and waiting at the tram stop. A tram rattled in my temples. It rattled like a box of matches. And the light inside the car flickered like a flame that you cup in your hand when it's windy outside. Lola's men pushed and shoved each other. Their bags disgorged detergent and the organ meats of slaughtered animals along the tracks. Then someone switched off the light, and the image in the windowpane disappeared, leaving only the yellow streetlights hanging in a row along the opposite side of the street. Then I was back among the girls standing around Lola's bed. There I heard a sound I will never forget or confuse with any other sound in the world. On the bed, beneath her back, I heard Lola mowing love that had never grown, blade by long blade on her dirty-white sheet.

The scabby pendulum struck inside my head as Lola panted, utterly beside herself.

There was only one of Lola's men I hadn't seen in the windowpane's reflection.

Lola went more and more often to the department head, and she still loved the title as much as ever. And although she said it more and more often, she still didn't realize how taken with the title she was. She talked more and more about consciousness and the convergence of town and country. For a week now Lola had belonged to the Party, and she produced her red book. The first page showed Lola's photograph. The Party book was passed from one girl's hand to the next. In the photograph I could see the poor province in Lola's face even more clearly, because the paper was so shiny. Someone said, But don't you go to church? And Lola said, The others do too. You just mustn't show that you recognize them there.

Someone said, God takes care of you up above and the Party takes care of you down below.

The Party leaflets piled up beside Lola's bed. Someone whispered in the little cube, and someone kept silent. For some time, the girls had been full of whispers and silences when Lola was in the room.

Lola writes in her notebook: Mother takes me to church. It's cold, but the priest's incense makes it seem warmer. All the people take their gloves off and hold them in their folded hands. I sit in the children's pew, at the very end, so I can see Mother.

Ever since Lola had taken to cleaning the glass display case, the girls made faces and hand gestures when there was something they didn't want to say in front of her.

Mother says she's praying for me too, writes Lola. My glove has a hole at the end of the thumb, the hole has a wreath of jagged stitches around it. To me it's a crown of thorns.

Lola sat on her bed and read a leaflet about delivering the Party's message more effectively.

I tug the thread, writes Lola, and the crown of thorns twists down. Mother sings, O God have mercy on us, and I unravel the thumb of my glove.

Lola underlined so many sentences in the thin leaflet, it was as if her hand were taking over. The pile of leaflets beside her bed grew like a crooked nightstand. While she was underlining, Lola would stop and think a long time between sentences.

I don't throw the wool away, writes Lola, even though it's all tangled.

Lola drew parentheses around the sentences in the leaflets. Beside every parenthesis, Lola drew a heavy cross in the margin.

Mother is knitting my thumb back, writes Lola, with new wool for the tip.

One afternoon when Lola was in her fourth year of study, all the girls' clothes were spread out on their beds. Lola's suitcase lay gaping under the open window, and her few clothes and all her leaflets were in the suitcase.

That afternoon I learned why there was one of Lola's men I hadn't been able to see in the reflecting window. He was different from all the other men, the midnight men, the late-shift men. He ate in the Party College, he never used the tram, he never followed Lola into the scruffy park, he had a car and a driver.

Lola writes in her notebook: He's my first man with a white shirt.

This is how it was that afternoon just before three o'clock, when Lola was already in her fourth year of study and had almost made something of herself: The girls' clothes lay on their beds, away from Lola's. The sun fell hot into the room, and dust covered the linoleum like gray fur. Next to Lola's bed, where the leaflets were no longer piled, was an empty, dark patch of floor. And Lola was hanging by my belt inside the closet.

Three men showed up. They photographed Lola in the closet. Then they untied the belt and placed it in a transparent plastic bag. It was as whisper-thin as the girls' nylons.

The men took three little boxes out of their jacket pockets. They shut the lid of Lola's suitcase and opened their boxes. Each was full of a venomous-green dust. They sprinkled it over the suitcase and then on the closet door. The powder was as dry as our mascara without the spit. I watched along with the other girls. I was surprised there was such a thing as venomous-green mascara.

The men didn't ask us a thing. They knew why she'd done it.

Five girls stood by the entrance of the dormitory. Inside the glass display case was Lola's picture, the same as the one in her Party book. Under the picture was a piece of paper. Someone read out loud:

This student has committed suicide. We abhor her crime and we despise her for it. She has brought disgrace upon the whole country.

Late in the afternoon, I found Lola's notebook in my suitcase. She had hidden it among my nylons before she took my belt.

I put the notebook in my handbag and walked to the tram stop. I got on the tram and read. I started on the last page. Lola writes: In the evening the gym teacher called me into the gym and locked the door from the inside. Only the leather medicine balls were watching. Once would have been enough for him. But I secretly followed him home. It will be impossible to keep his shirts white. He reported me to the department head. I will never escape the drought. God will not pardon me for what I have to do. But no child of mine will ever drive sheep with red shanks.

That evening I secretly put Lola's notebook back in my suitcase, under the nylons. I locked the suitcase and put the key under my pillow. In the morning I took the key with me. I knotted it into the elastic of my underpants because we had a gym class first thing, at eight. I was a little late because of the key.

The girls, in black shorts and white gym shirts, were already standing in a row at the head of the sandpit. Two girls stood at the far end and held the tape measure. The wind drove into the thick foliage of the trees. The gym teacher raised his arm, snapped his fingers, and the girls all flew through the air feet first.

The sand in the pit was dry. Only where your toes dug into it was it damp. It felt as cool to my toes as the key against my belly. I looked up into the trees before I started my run. I flew feet first, but my feet didn't fly very far. As I was flying I thought about my suitcase key. The two girls put down the tape measure and called out the distance. The gym teacher recorded the jump in his book. I saw the sharpened pencil in his hand and thought, that's him, all right, the only thing that can be measured at the far end is death.

When I went flying for the second time, the key had grown as warm as my skin. It didn't press anymore. When my toes dug into the damp sand, I got up quickly, so that the gym instructor couldn't touch me.

24

• • •

At four o'clock in the afternoon, in the great hall, two days after she'd hanged herself, Lola was expelled from the Party and exmatriculated from the university. Hundreds of people were there.

Someone stood at the lectern and said: She deceived us all, she doesn't deserve to be a student in our country or a member of our Party. Everybody applauded.

In the cube that evening someone said: Everyone felt like crying, but couldn't, so they applauded too long instead. No one dared to be the first to stop. Everybody looked at each other's hands while they were clapping. A few people stopped for a moment, then were so frightened they started clapping all over again. By that time most of the people wanted to stop, you could hear the clapping in the room lose its rhythm, but because those few had started again, everyone else had to keep going. At last, when one beat bounced against the walls like a giant shoe, the speaker raised his hand for silence.

Lola's picture hung in the display case for two weeks. But after two days Lola's notebook had disappeared from my locked suitcase.

The men with the venomous-green mascara laid Lola on her bed and carried it out of the cube. Why did they carry the bed through the door feet first? One of the men followed carrying the suitcase with her clothes and the bag with my belt. He carried the suitcase and the belt in his right hand. Why didn't he shut the door after him? His left hand was free.

Five girls were left in the cube, five beds, five suitcases. When Lola's bed was gone, someone shut the door. With every movement in the room, the threads of dust twisted together in the hot, bright air. Someone stood against the wall, combing her hair. Someone shut the window. Someone re-laced her shoes in a different way.

None of the movements in the room had any purpose. Everyone was silent and busied herself with her hands, since no one dared take the clothes off her own bed and hang them back up in the closet.

Mother says: Whenever life becomes unbearable, clean your closet. Then your worries will go out through your hands, and that will free your head.

But that's easy for her to say. She has five wardrobes in her house and five chests. And even when Mother straightens up her chests and wardrobes for three days without stopping, it still looks as if there's more work to be done.

I went into the scruffy park and dropped the suitcase key in the bushes. There was no key to protect my suitcase against unknown hands when none of the girls was in the room. Maybe there wasn't even any key to protect against more familiar hands, hands that stirred the mascara with tooth-picks, that switched the lights on and off, or that, after Lola's death, scrubbed the iron clean.

Perhaps no one need have resorted to whispers and silence when Lola was in the room. Perhaps someone could have told Lola everything. Perhaps I in particular could have told Lola everything. The suitcase lock had made a lie of itself. There were as many identical suitcase keys in the country as there were workers' choruses. Every key was a lie.

When I returned from the park, someone in the cube was singing for the first time since Lola's death:

Late last night a gust of wind
drove me to my lover's arms
Had it gusted any harder
it would have snapped his arm in two
good thing that the wind stood still.

Someone sang a Romanian song. Through the night within the song, I saw sheep wandering with red shanks. I heard in that song how the wind stood still.

A child lies in bed saying: Don't turn out the light, or else the black trees will come in. A grandmother comes and tucks the child in. Go to sleep quickly, she says; once everybody's asleep, the wind will lie down in the trees. In this children's bedtime language, the wind could never stand still, it could only lie down.

. . .

After the applause in the great hall had died down at a signal from the rector, the gym instructor stepped up to the rostrum. He was wearing a white shirt. A vote was taken on whether to expel Lola from the Party and to exmatriculate her from the university.

The gym instructor was the first to raise his hand. All the other hands flew up after his. While raising their hands, everybody looked at the raised hands of the others. If someone's own hand wasn't as high as the others', he would stretch his arm a little farther. People kept their hands up until their fingers grew tired and started to droop and their elbows began to feel heavy and pull downward. Everyone looked around, and since no one else's arm was lowered, they straightened their fingers again and extended their elbows. Sweat stains showed under the arms; shirts and blouses came untucked. Necks were stretched, ears turned red, lips parted and stayed half-open. Heads kept still, while eyes slid from side to side.

It was so quiet among the hands, someone said inside the cube, that you could hear the breathing up and down the wooden benches. And it stayed that quiet until the gym instructor laid his arm across the lectern and said: There's no need to count, of course we're all in favor.

All these people walking up and down these streets, I thought in town the following day, would have vaulted the horse in the great hall at the gym instructor's signal. All these people would have straightened their fingers, extended their elbows, and their eyes would have slid from side to side in the silence. I counted all the faces I passed in the stabbing hot sun. Up to nine hundred and ninety-nine. By then the soles of my feet were burning, I sat down on a bench, curled my toes, and propped up my back. I pressed my finger against my cheek and counted myself in, too. One thousand, I said to myself, and swallowed the number.

A pigeon ran past the bench, and I watched it. It trotted along, trailing its wings. Its beak was half-open because of the heat.

It pecked and made a noise as if its beak were made of tin. It gobbled down a pebble. And as the pigeon swallowed the pebble I thought: Lola would have raised her hand, too. But that didn't count anymore.

I watched Lola's men as they came off the early shift in the factories. They were peasants, fetched here from their villages. They, too, had said to themselves, no more sheep, no more melons. Like fools, they had gone chasing after the soot of the city, following the thick pipes that crept across the fields to the edge of every village.

The men knew that their iron, their wood, and their detergent didn't count. That's why their hands remained crude, that's why they manufactured lumps and clods instead of craft and industry. All that was supposed to be great and sharp-edged became a tin sheep in their hands. All that was supposed to be little and round, became in their hands a wooden melon.

The proletariat of tin sheep and wooden melons headed for the nearest bar as soon as their shift was over. Always in a herd, they would crowd into the garden of a bodega. As they dumped their heavy bodies onto the chairs, the waiter turned over the red tablecloth. Corks, breadcrusts, and bones were scattered onto the ground next to a tub of flowers. The greenery was dried out, the earth scarred by cigarettes quickly extinguished. On the fence of the bodega hung geranium pots full of naked stalks. Three or four budding leaves were unfolding at the tips.

The fodder steamed on the tables, which were cluttered with hands holding spoons, never knives or forks. Pulling and tearing with their teeth, that was how everyone ate, when the organ meats of slaughtered beasts lay on the platters.

The bodega, too, was a lie, with its tablecloths and plants, its bottles and the wine-red uniforms of its waiters. Here no one was a guest, they were all just refugees from a meaningless afternoon.

The men staggered and yelled at one another before smashing each other over the head with empty bottles. They bled. If a tooth fell to the ground, they would laugh as if someone had lost a button. Someone would bend over, pick up the tooth, and toss it into his glass. Because it brought good luck, the tooth was passed from glass to glass. Everyone wanted it.

At some point the tooth disappeared, it vanished like Lola's tongues and kidneys from the common fridge. At some point one of the men would have swallowed it. None of them knew who. They tore the last of the budding young leaves off the geranium stalks and chewed them suspiciously. They checked all the glasses, one after the other, and shouted, with their mouths full of green leaves: It's plums you should be eating, not teeth.

They pointed at someone, they all pointed at the one in a light-green shirt. He denied it. He stuck his finger down his throat. He vomited and said: Now you can see for yourselves, there are geranium leaves, meat, bread, and beer, but no tooth. The waiters threw him out, while the others all clapped.

Then someone in a checked shirt said: It was me. As he laughed, he began to cry. Everyone went quiet and stared down at the table. Here no one was a guest.

Peasants, I thought—only peasants jump from laughing to crying, from shouting to silence. They were beside themselves, blindly happy and bursting with rage. So great was their desire for life that each passing moment was capable of extinguishing life in one blow. Every one of them would have followed Lola into the bushes in the dark, with the same doggish eyes.

If they stayed sober the following day, they would go into the park alone to get a grip on themselves. Their lips would be parched and white from booze, the corners of their mouths cracked. They would step cautiously on the grass, chewing over every word they had shouted while drunk. They would crawl into the lost memories of the previous day and sit there like children. They were scared they might have shouted something political in the bodega. They knew the waiters reported everything.

But booze protects the skull from the forbidden, and fodder protects the mouth. Even when the tongue can only babble, the habit of fear does not desert the voice.

They were at home in their fear. The factory and the bodega, the shops and the apartment blocks, the railway stations and the train rides through fields of wheat, corn, and sunflowers all were listening. The streetcars, the hospitals, and the graveyards. The walls and the ceilings and the open sky. And if it happened, as it often did, that drunkenness grew careless in places which were lies, it was more like a mistake on the part of the walls or the ceilings or the open sky, than any intention of the human brain.

And while the mother is tying the child to the chair with the belt of her dress, while the barber is cutting the grandfather's hair, while the father is telling the child not to eat green plums, during all these years, a grandmother is standing in the corner of the room. She follows all the comings and goings so absentmindedly, as if the wind had lain down that morning, as if the day had fallen asleep in the sky. Throughout all those years, Grandmother hums a tune to herself.

The child has two grandmothers. One brings her love to the child at bedtime, and the child looks up at the white ceiling because she knows that Grandmother is about to start praying. The other brings her love to the child at bedtime, and the child gazes into her dark eyes, because she knows that Grandmother is about to start singing.

When the child can no longer bear the sight of the ceiling or the dark eyes, she pretends to sleep. The first grandmother doesn't finish her prayer. She gets up in the middle and walks out. The other grandmother finishes her song, her face is crooked because she loves singing so much.

When her song is finished, she thinks the child is fast

asleep. She says: Rest your heart-beast now, you've played so much today.

The singing grandmother outlives the praying grandmother by nine years. And she outlives her own reason by six years. She no longer recognizes anyone in the house. All she remembers are her songs.

One evening she walks from the corner of the room to the table and says, in the glow of the light, I'm so glad you're all with me in Heaven. She doesn't realize she's alive and that she'll have to sing herself to death. No illness will come to help her die.

For two years after Lola's death I didn't wear a belt with my dresses. The loudest sounds of the city seemed quiet inside my head. Whenever a truck or a tram approached, the rattling felt good in my forehead. The ground shook underfoot. I wanted to have something to do with the wheels and dashed across the road at the last moment. I took a chance on whether I reached the other side or not. I let the wheels decide for me. The dust swallowed me for a while, my hair fluttered between luck and death. I reached the other side and laughed; I had won. But I heard my laughter from outside and from a long way off.

I often went to the shop that had aluminum bowls full of tongue and liver and kidney in its windows. The shop was never on my way, I had to take the tram. The provinces in people's faces reached their greatest size inside the shop. Men and women carried bags of cucumbers and onions. But I saw them carrying mulberry trees out of their provinces and into their faces. I would choose someone no older than myself and set off after him. I always ended up at the apartment blocks of some new settlement, always passed through high thistles to end up in a village. In among the thistles were patches of screaming-red tomatoes and white turnips. Each patch was a piece of failed field. I only saw the eggplants when my shoes were almost on top of them. They gleamed like double handfuls of black mulberries.

The world hasn't waited for anyone, I thought. I didn't have to walk, eat, sleep, and love someone in fear. I didn't need the barber, and I didn't need the nail-clippers, I didn't lose any buttons before there was me. Father was still caught up in the war and lived from singing and shooting in the grass. He didn't have to love. The grass should have kept him. Because when he came back from the war and saw the village sky, a farmer grew back into his shirt and took up his handiwork again. The survivor had made graveyards, and had to make me.

I became his child and had to grow against death. I was hissed at, not spoken to. They slapped my hands and looked me right in the eye to see how I took it. But no one ever asked me in what house, in what place, at what table, in which bed and country I would prefer to walk, eat, sleep, or love someone in fear.

Always tying, never untying, since that took too long to become a word. I wanted to speak about Lola, and the girls in the cube told me to shut up. They realized that their heads were lighter without Lola. A table and chair now stood in the cube where Lola's bed had been. And on the table, a big preserving jar with long sprays from the scruffy park, dwarf white roses with delicately serrated leaves. The branches put down white roots in the water. The girls could walk and eat and sleep in the cube. They weren't afraid to sing in front of Lola's leaves.

I wanted to keep Lola's notebook in my head.

Edgar, Kurt, and Georg were looking for someone who shared Lola's room. After they approached me in the cafeteria, I met with them every day: I couldn't keep Lola's notebook in my head on my own. They doubted whether Lola's death was suicide.

I told them about the leaf-fleas, the sheep with red shanks, the mulberry trees, and the province in Lola's face. When I thought of Lola on my own, there were many things I could no longer remember. When they were listening, everything came back to me. I learned from their staring eyes how to read what was in my head.

In the crevices of my skull I found every missing sentence from Lola's notebook. I would say each out loud. And Edgar wrote many sentences in his own notebook. I said: Your notebook will disappear soon too, because Edgar, Kurt, and Georg all lived in a dormitory on the other side of the scruffy park, a dormitory for boys. But Edgar said: We have a safe place in town, a summerhouse in an overgrown garden.

We'll put the notebook in a sack, said Kurt, and hang it from the underside of the lid of the well. They all laughed and kept saying: We. Georg said: From a little hook. The well is indoors, the summerhouse and the overgrown garden belong to a man who attracts no suspicion. The books are there too, said Kurt.

The books in the summerhouse came from far away, but they knew about every province in the faces of this city, every tin sheep, every wooden melon. Every bout of drunkenness, every laugh in the bodega.

Who is the man with the summerhouse? I asked, and thought right away: I don't want to know. Edgar, Kurt, and Georg all kept quiet. Their eyes were crooked, and in the white corners of their eyes, where the little veins run together, their silence glistened uneasily. I told them about the great hall, the beat of a giant shoe that climbed up the wall as the hands kept applauding. And about the breath that crawled along the wooden benches when the arms were raised to be counted.

And I felt as I talked that there was something like a cherrystone on my tongue. Truth was waiting for me to count myself, for my finger against my own cheek. But the words one thousand didn't pass my lips. Nor did I say anything about the tin beak of the pigeon that was pecking at pebbles. I went on about the gymnastic horse and flying into the sand, about being touched and being given water, about the suitcase key attached to the elastic of my underpants. Edgar listened with his pen in his hand and didn't write a single word in his notebook. And I thought to myself: He's still waiting for the truth, he can sense that for all my talk,

I'm keeping something quiet. And then I said: He's my first man with a white shirt. And Edgar wrote it down. And then I said: We all have leaves. And Georg said: You can't wrap your brain around that.

You could say Lola's sentences in your mouth. But they didn't let themselves be written down. Not by me. They were like dreams, suited for speech but not for paper. When I wrote them down, Lola's sentences dissolved in my hand.

The books in the summerhouse had more in them than I was used to thinking about. I took them to the graveyard and sat on a bench. Old people came, one by one, to visit a grave that would soon be theirs too. They brought no flowers, the graves were covered with them anyway. They didn't weep, they stared into space. Sometimes one would search for a handkerchief, bend down and wipe the dust off his shoes, retie the laces, and tuck the handkerchief away again. They didn't weep because they didn't want to make work for their cheeks. Because each of their faces was already on a tombstone, cheek to cheek with the deceased in a round photograph. They had sent themselves on ahead and had been waiting since who knows when for the meeting on the tombstone to be made binding. Their names and dates of birth had been chiseled into the stone. A handsbreadth of unchiseled space waited for the date of death. They never stayed long at the grave.

The tombstones and I watched them as they walked away down the narrow paths bordered with flowers. After they had left the graveyard, the many smooth spaces linked themselves to the summer day, which was heavy and sluggish from the mounds of flowers. Here, out of the city, summer grew differently. The graveyard summer didn't care for hot wind. It quietly pushed up the sky and kept a lookout for fatalities. In town people said: Spring and fall are risky for old folk. The first warmth and the first chill carry them off. But here you could see that summer set the trap best. It was summer who knew how to turn old folk into flowers, day after day.

Leaves grow back when you shrivel up because love is all gone, Lola writes in her notebook.

With Lola's sentences inside my head, I breathed gently, so that the sentences from the books didn't stumble because they were behind Lola's leaves.

I had learned how to wander, I walked the streets. I knew the beggars, the wailing voices, the signs of the cross, and the curses, God naked and the devil in rags, the crippled hands and half-legs.

I knew the demented in every part of town.

The man with the black bow tie around his neck, always holding the same withered bouquet. For years he'd been standing by the dry fountain, looking up the street at the other end of which was the prison. When I spoke to him, he said: I can't talk now, she'll be coming any moment, maybe she won't recognize me anymore.

She'll be coming any moment, he'd been saying for years. And sometimes when he said it, someone did come down the street, a policeman or a soldier. As for his wife, the whole city knew she had left prison long ago. She was in the graveyard, in her tomb.

At seven in the morning a column of buses with their gray curtains drawn drove down the street. And at seven at night, it drove back up. The street didn't actually run uphill, the end of it wasn't any higher than the square with the fountain. But that's how people saw it. Or maybe they just said it ran uphill because that's where the prison was, and only policemen and soldiers ever went there.

As the buses drove past the fountain, you could see the fingers of the prisoners through gaps in the curtains. There was no sound from the moving engines, no revving or rumbling, no brakes or wheels. Only the barking of the dogs. That was so loud, it was as though twice a day dogs on wheels drove past the fountain.

First the horses on high heels, and now the dogs on wheels.

A mother takes the train into the city every week. The child is allowed to accompany her twice a year. Once at the beginning of summer, and once at the beginning of winter. The child feels ugly in town, because she's bundled up in so much thick clothing. The mother takes the child to the station at four in the morning. It's cold, even in early summer it's still cold at four in the morning. The mother wants to be in the city by eight, because that's when the stores open.

From one store to the next, the child pulls off some of her

clothes and carries them in her hand. As a result, the child loses a few items of clothing in the city. That's why the mother doesn't like taking the child into town. But there's another reason: The child sees horses trotting on the asphalt. The child stops and wants her mother to stop, too, and wait for more horses to come. The mother has no time to wait and can't go on by herself. She doesn't want to lose the child in the city. She has to drag the child away. The child hangs back and says: Do you hear how the hooves clatter differently from at home?

From one store to the next, in the train on the way home, and for days after, the child asks: Why do horses in the city wear high heels?

I knew the dwarf lady on Trajan Square. She had more scalp than hair, she was deaf and dumb, and she wore a grass pigtail like the discarded chairs underneath the old people's mulberry trees. She lived off the rubbish from the greengrocer's shop. Every year she got pregnant by Lola's men, who came off the late shift at midnight. It was dark in the square. The dwarf lady couldn't run away in time, because she couldn't hear their approach. And she couldn't scream.

The philosopher's beat was around the station. He mistook telephone poles and tree trunks for people. He talked to wood and iron about Kant and the universe of ravenous sheep. In the bodegas he went from table to table, draining the dregs from the glasses and wiping them dry with his long, white beard.

In front of the marketplace sat the old woman whose hat was fashioned out of newspapers and pins. For years she'd pulled a sled laden with sacks through the streets, winter and summer. One sack contained folded newspapers. The old woman made herself a new hat each day. Another sack contained the hats she'd already worn.

Only the demented would not have raised their hands in the great hall. They had exchanged fear for insanity.

I, on the other hand, could go on counting people in the streets, go on counting myself, too, as if I might run into myself by chance. I could say to myself: Hey, you, someone. Or: Hey, you, one thousand. The only thing I couldn't do was go insane. I was still in my right mind.

To quiet my hunger, I bought myself something I could eat as I walked. I'd sooner tear meat apart with my teeth on the street than at a table in the cafeteria. I no longer went to the cafeteria. I sold my meal ticket and bought three pairs of whisper-thin nylons with the proceeds.

Now I only went into the cube in order to sleep, but I didn't sleep. My head became transparent when I laid it on the pillow in the darkened room. The window was bright with the glow from the streetlamps. I saw my head in the windowpane, the roots of my hair planted in my scalp like tiny onions. If I turn over, I thought, my hair will fall out. But I had to turn over, so as not to see the window anymore.

Then I was facing the door. Even if the man with Lola's suitcase and my belt in the transparent plastic bag had shut the door behind him, death would still have stayed here in the room. At night, in the glow from the streetlamps, the closed door was Lola's bed.

All the others were fast asleep. Between my head and the pillow, I heard the dry objects of the mad people rustling: the withered bouquet of the waiting man, the grass pigtail of the dwarf lady, the newspaper hat of the old sled woman, the philosopher's white beard.

At his midday meal, the grandfather puts his fork down when he finishes the last bite. He gets up from the table and says: One hundred paces. He walks, counting his paces. He walks from the table to the door, across the threshold, into the courtyard, along the path, and onto the grass. The child thinks he's going away now, he's going into the woods.

Then the hundred paces are up. The grandfather comes back, without counting, over the grass and onto the path, across the threshold, up to the table. He sits down and sets up his chess pieces, the two queens last. He plays chess. He spreads his elbows on the table, he tugs at his hair, he drums a quick rhythm with his feet under the table, he moves his tongue from cheek to cheek, he crosses his arms. Grandfather becomes sullen and lonely. The room disappears, because the grandfather is playing against himself, with both the dark pieces and the light ones. The farther his meal travels from his mouth to his bowels, the more wrinkled his face becomes. So lonely that he has to quiet all his memories of the First World War with the dark and the light queens.

Grandfather had returned from the First World War just as from his hundred paces. In Italy they have snakes as thick as my arm, he said. They roll themselves up like cartwheels. They lie on stones between villages, and sleep. I sat down on one of those cartwheels, and the company barber rubbed the bald patches on my head with leaf extract.

Grandfather's chess pieces were the size of his thumbs. But the queens were as tall as his middle fingers. Each had a little black stone under the left shoulder. I asked: Why do they have only one breast? Grandfather said: The little stones are their hearts. I saved the queens till last, said Grandfather, I carved them after all the other pieces. I fussed over them a long time. The company barber had told me: There's no leaf on earth to save the hairs still on your head. There's no hope for them: they'll just have to leave your head. It's only the bald patches I can do anything about; only there does the leaf extract force the head to make new hair.

By the time the queens were finished, I had lost all my hair, Grandfather said.

Edgar, Kurt, Georg, and I were watching the proletariat of tin sheep and wooden melons going on and coming off their shifts. We were talking about how we had each left home. Edgar and I came from the country, Kurt and Georg from small towns.

I talked about the sacks of mulberry trees, about the old people in their courtyards, and about Lola's notebook: Out of the province and into the face. Edgar nodded and Georg said: Everyone's a villager here. Our heads may have left home, but our feet are just standing in a different village. No cities can grow in a dictatorship, because everything stays small when it's being watched.

You travel from city to city, said Georg, and you become first one villager and then another villager. Kurt said: You can even leave yourself completely out of it; you get on the train, and it's just one village traveling to another village.

When I left, Edgar said, fields rolled from the village all the way to the city. The corn was still green and cool. I thought our kitchen garden had stretched itself out and was chasing the train. The train moved slowly.

To me it felt like a long journey and a great distance, I said. The sunflowers had no more leaves, and their black stalks seemed to measure the distance. They had such black seeds that the people in my compartment grew tired looking at them. Everyone in the compartment was overcome by sleep. One woman held a gray goose on her lap. The woman had fallen asleep, and the goose chattered awhile longer on her lap. Then it laid its neck on its wings and went to sleep too.

The forest kept covering the window, Kurt said, so when I suddenly saw a strip of sky, I thought, There's a river up ahead. The forest had erased the whole region. That matched the inside of my father's head. He was so drunk when we said goodbye, he thought his son was going to war. He laughed and slapped my mother on the shoulder and said: Now our Kurt's off to the war. My mother screamed when he said

44

that. She screamed and then she started crying. How can you be so drunk? she screamed. But she was crying because she believed what he was saying.

My father pushed his bicycle along between us, Georg said. I carried my suitcase. As the train left the station, I saw my father walking back to town with his bicycle. A dash and a dot.

My father is superstitious, my mother's always sewing him green jackets. If you don't wear green, the forest will bury you, he says. His camouflage doesn't come from any beast, said Kurt, it comes from the war.

My father, said Georg, took his bicycle to the station so that he wouldn't have to walk so close to me on the way there, and so that, on the way back, his empty hands wouldn't remind him he was returning home alone.

The mothers of Edgar, Kurt, and Georg were all seamstresses. They all lived surrounded by stiff canvas, linings, scissors, thread, needles, buttons, and irons. When Edgar, Kurt, and Georg told me about their mothers' illnesses, it seemed to me as if seamstresses were somehow softened up by the steam from their irons. They were all sick on the inside: Edgar's mother in her gallbladder, Kurt's mother in her stomach, and Georg's mother in her spleen.

My mother, though, was a peasant and had been toughened by the fields. She was sick on the outside, in the small of her back.

When we talked about our mothers, rather than our SS-fathers who had come back from the war, we were amazed that our mothers, who had never met in their lives, all sent us the same letters, full of their illnesses.

By trains that we no longer boarded ourselves, each sent

us the pain of her gallbladder, her stomach, her spleen, her back. These illnesses had been lifted out of our mothers' bodies and lay inside the letters like the stolen organ meats of slaughtered beasts inside the compartment of the fridge.

Our illnesses, our mothers thought to themselves, are a knot with which to tie our children. Even though they're far away they will remain tightly tied to us. How they wished for a child who would find the train, ride through sunflower fields or forests, and show its face at home.

Our mothers hoped to see a face that showed tightly tied love in cheek or brow. They wished to see the first few wrinkles, signs that our life as grown-ups was harder for us than our childhood had been.

But they forgot that they were no longer permitted to stroke or slap this face. That they could no longer touch it.

Our mothers' illnesses sensed that, for us, untying was a beautiful word.

We were no different from those who brought mulberry trees with them, but we only half-admitted it in our conversations. We looked for things that would set us apart because we read books. While we drew tiny distinctions, we stored all the sacks we had brought behind our doors, just like everyone else.

But in our books we learned that those doors were no shelter. All we could open or slam or leave ajar were our own foreheads. And behind those were ourselves, with our mothers who sent us their illnesses in letters and our fathers who stashed their guilty consciences inside the damn stupid plants.

The books in the summerhouse had been smuggled into the country. They were written in German, our mother tongue, the one in which the wind lay down. Not the official language of the country. But not quite the children's bedtime language of the village either. The books were in our mother tongue, but the silence of the villages, which forbids thought, wasn't in them. We imagined the land where the books came from as a land of thinkers. We sniffed at the pages and caught ourselves sniffing our own hands out of habit. We were surprised our hands didn't blacken as we read, the way they did from the ink in the newspapers and books printed in our country.

All the people who went around the city carrying their provinces with them sniffed at their hands. They didn't know the books from the summerhouse. But they wanted to go there. In the land those books came from, there were bluejeans and oranges, soft toys for children and portable TVs for fathers and whisper-thin nylons and real mascara for mothers.

Everyone lived by thinking about flight. They thought of swimming across the Danube until the water becomes another country. Of running after the corn until the soil becomes another country. You could see it in their eyes: Soon they will spend every penny they have on detailed maps.

They hope for fog in the field and fog on the river for days on end so they can avoid the bullets and the guard dogs, so they can run away, swim away. You could see it in their hands: Soon they will build balloons, fragile birds made of bedsheets and saplings. They hope the wind won't drop, so they can fly away. You could see it on their lips: Soon they will whisper to a stationmaster in exchange for every penny they have. They will climb onto freight trains so they can roll away.

The only ones who didn't want to flee were the dictator and his guards. You could see it in their eyes, hands, lips: Today and tomorrow and the next day they will make grave-yards, with dogs and with bullets. But also with the belt, the nut, the window, and the rope.

You could feel the dictator and his guards hovering over all the secret escape plans, you could feel them lurking and doling out fear.

In the evening the light at the end of every street quivered. It was an insistent light, warning the surroundings that night was coming. The houses became smaller than the people who were passing by them. The bridges smaller than the trams that were driving over them. And the trees smaller than the faces that, one by one, were walking beneath them.

Everywhere was a way home, and everything was a thoughtless rush. The few faces on the street had no edge. I saw a wisp of cloud in them as they came toward me. And when they were almost in front of me, they shriveled up at the next step. Only the paving stones kept their size. And at the very next step, instead of the cloud, were two white eyeballs in a forehead. And at the step after, just before the faces were behind me, the two eyeballs melted together.

I stuck to the ends of the streets, where it was lighter. Where the clouds were nothing but bundles of crumpled clothes. I wanted to drag things out, because the only bed I had was in the cube with the girls. I wanted to wait for the girls in the cube to be asleep. In the bleak light I had no choice but to walk, and I walked faster and faster. The side streets weren't waiting for nightfall. They were already packing their suitcases.

Edgar and Georg wrote poetry and hid it in the summerhouse. Kurt lurked in corners and in bushes, photographing the columns of buses with their gray curtains drawn. Every morning and evening they drove the prisoners from the prison to the construction sites beyond the fields. It's so creepy, said Kurt, that you expect to hear the dogs barking in the photographs. If the dogs barked in the photographs, Edgar said, we wouldn't be able to hide the photographs in the summerhouse.

And I thought to myself that everything that harms the graveyard makers was useful. That Edgar, Kurt, and Georg, by writing poems and taking pictures and now and again humming a tune, would inspire hatred in the graveyard makers. That such hatred would harm the guards. That little by little this hatred could make all the guards—and finally even the dictator himself—lose their heads.

I didn't know yet that the guards needed that hatred to perform their bloody work with daily precision. That they needed it to pass judgments in return for their wages. They could only pass judgments on their enemies. The guards proved their reliability by the number of their enemies.

Edgar said, The secret police itself spreads the rumors about the dictator's illnesses, in order to get people to flee and then catch them. To get people to whisper and then catch them. It's not enough to catch people stealing meat or matches, corn or detergent, candles or screws, hairclips or nails or planks.

As I wandered, I didn't only see the demented and their dried-up belongings. I also saw the guards walking up and down the streets. Young men with yellowish teeth standing guard at the entrances of big buildings, outside shops, on squares, at tramstops, in the scruffy park, in front of the dormitories, in bodegas, outside the station. Their suits fitted them badly; they were either too loose or too tight. They knew where the plum trees were in every precinct they policed. They even took roundabout routes to pass by the plum trees. The boughs drooped. The guards filled their pockets with green plums. They picked them fast, their pockets bulged. One picking was supposed to last them a long time. After they had filled their jacket pockets, they quickly left the trees behind. Plumsucker was a term of abuse. Upstarts, opportunists, sycophants, and people who stepped over dead bodies without remorse were called that. The dictator was called a plumsucker, too.

The young men walked up and down and reached their hands inside their jacket pockets. They took the plums out a fistful at a time, to attract attention less often. Only when their mouths were full could they close their fists.

Because they always took so many plums at once, one or two always fell on the ground or rolled down their sleeves while they ate. The guards kicked the plums that fell on the ground into the grass, like little balls. They fished the other plums from the crooks of their elbows and stuffed them into their already bulging cheeks.

I saw the foam on their teeth and thought: You can't eat green plums, the pits are still soft, and you'll swallow your death.

The plumsuckers were peasants. The green plums made them stupid. They ate themselves away from their duty. They reverted to childhood, stealing plums from village trees. They didn't eat because they were hungry, they just lusted after the sour taste of the poverty which had so recently ruled their lives, a strict father before whom they had cast down their eyes and bowed their heads.

They emptied their jacket pockets, smoothed out the bulges, and hauled the plums around in their bellies. They didn't burn up with fever. They were oversized children. Far away from home, the inner heat was burned off as duty.

They would shout at one person because the sun was burning, the wind was blowing, or the rain was falling. They would grab another by the lapels and then let him go. They would beat up a third. Sometimes the heat from the plums lay quietly in their heads, and they would arrest a fourth person, with determination and without rage. Fifteen minutes later they would be back at their posts.

When a young woman passed, they would stare at her legs. The decision to grab her or let her go was always made at the last minute. They wanted to make it obvious that legs like that didn't need a reason—just a whim.

People walked past them quickly and quietly. They recognized one another from before. That's why they walked so quietly. The clocks rang from church towers, dividing sunny and rainy days alike into mornings and afternoons. The sky changed its light, the asphalt its color, the wind its direction, the trees their murmur.

Edgar, Kurt, and Georg had also eaten green plums when they were children. They didn't have any association with plums, because their fathers hadn't told them not to eat them. They laughed at me when I said: No one can help then, you just die. The raging fever will burn up your heart from the inside. They shook their heads when I said: I didn't have to swallow my death, because my father didn't see me eating. The guards eat out in the open, I said. They don't swallow their deaths because the passersby know the sound of the snapping twigs and the sour belch of poverty.

Edgar, Kurt, and Georg lived in the same dormitory, each in a different room. Edgar on the fifth floor, Kurt on the third, Georg on the fourth. In each room there were five boys, five beds, five suitcases stowed away underneath the beds. A window, a loudspeaker over the door, a closet built into the wall. Each suitcase contained socks, and under the socks were shaving cream and a razor.

When Edgar walked into the room, someone threw his shoes out the window and shouted: Why don't you just jump out after them and put them on in midair? On the third floor, someone slammed Kurt against the closet door and shouted: Take your crap elsewhere. On the fourth floor, Georg caught a leaflet in the face, and someone shouted: If you're gonna make shit, then eat it yourself.

The boys threatened to beat up Edgar, Kurt, and Georg. Three men had just been and gone. They had searched the rooms and told the boys: If you don't want any more visits from us, talk to the person who isn't here. Talk to him they said, and waved their fists.

When Edgar, Kurt, and Georg walked into their oblongs, the preordained fury collapsed. Edgar laughed and threw a suitcase out the window. Kurt said: Watch out, you maggot. Georg said: You talk about shit, your own teeth are rotting in your mouth.

In each room, it was only one of the four other boys who was really angry, reported Edgar, Kurt, and Georg. The rage dissipated, because the other three had decided on the same thing, and left the angry one in the lurch when Edgar, Kurt, and Georg appeared. They stood there, as though extinguished.

The angry boy from Edgar's room slammed the door behind him. He ran downstairs and came back with his suitcase, he also brought back Edgar's shoes.

There wasn't a lot to search in the little oblong, Edgar said: They didn't find anything. And Georg said: They stirred up the fleas, the sheets are full of little black smudges. The boys sleep badly, and walk around the room at night.

There was a lot to search in the homes of Edgar, Kurt, and Georg's parents. Georg's mother sent him a letter with the pain in her spleen, which had grown through her fear. Kurt's mother sent him a letter with the pain in her stomach, which was raging. For the first time, the fathers each wrote a line in the margin, saying: Don't ever do that to your mother again.

Edgar's father took the train into the city, and boarded a tram. He got off the tram and took a roundabout way to the dormitory, avoiding the scruffy park. He asked a boy to have Edgar come down from his room to the front door.

Edgar said, When I was going down the steps and spotted my father at the bottom, I saw a little boy reading the announcements in the glass display case. What is there to read? I said, and he gave me a bag of freshly picked hazelnuts from home. He took a letter from my mother out of his breast pocket and said: The park has gone to ruin, no one likes to go there anymore. Edgar nodded and read in the letter that the pain in her gallbladder had become unbearable.

Edgar and his father walked through the park to the bodega behind the tram stop.

Three men in a car, said Edgar's father. One of them

stayed out on the street. He sat down beside the ditch and waited, he was just the driver. Two came inside. The younger one was bald, the older one was already gray. Edgar's mother wanted to pull up the blinds in the room, and the bald one said: Leave them down and turn on the light. The older one stripped the bed and searched the pillows, the blankets, the mattress. He demanded a screwdriver. The bald one unscrewed the bedstead.

Edgar walked slowly, and his father limped beside him on the path. As he talked, he peered into the undergrowth as though to count the leaves. Edgar asked: What are you looking for? His father said: They rolled up the carpet and emptied the cupboards. I'm not looking for anything, I haven't lost anything, have I?

Edgar pointed at his father's jacket. When his father took the letter out of his inside pocket, Edgar had already noticed a button missing. Edgar laughed: Maybe you're looking for your button. His father said: I bet I lost that on the train.

The men weren't able to read the letters from Edgar's two uncles in Austria and Brazil, said Edgar's father, because they were written in German. They took the letters with them. Also the photographs that were enclosed with the letters. The photographs of the two uncles' houses, their extended families, the families' houses. All the houses were the same. How many rooms do these Austrians have? asked the older man. And the bald one asked: What kind of trees are those? He pointed to a photograph from Brazil. Edgar's father shrugged his shoulders. Where are the letters to your son? asked the older one, the ones from his girl cousin. She's never written him any, said Edgar's mother. Are you sure? he asked. Edgar's mother said: No, maybe she does write him letters and they never reach him.

The older one emptied boxes of buttons and zippers onto the table. The bald one threw fabric, canvas, and linings in a heap. Edgar's father said: Your mother no longer has any idea what belongs to which of her customers. Who gave you that fashion magazine? they asked. Edgar's mother pointed to the briefcases where the letters and photographs were kept: That's from my brother in Austria. I hope you like stripes, said the older one, you'll be wearing them soon enough.

In the bodega, Edgar's father sat down carefully on the chair, as if someone were already sitting there. In Edgar's room, the bald one had ripped open the curtain hem, thrown the old books off the shelves, and shaken them out over the floor. Edgar's father pressed his hands down on the table to keep them from trembling. He said: What did they think was going to be in those old books anyway? The only thing that fell out was dust. He spilled some schnapps from the glass as he swallowed.

Edgar's father said: They tore the flowers out of the window box and ran the soil through their fingers. The dirt fell on the tablecloth, and the thin roots dangled between their fingers. The bald one puzzled some words of German out of the cookbook: *Brasilianische Leber: Hühnerleber in Mehl pudern*—liver Brazilian style, dredge chicken livers in flour, Edgar's mother had to translate. You'll be getting soup, he said, with a couple of bull's eyes swimming in it. The older one went out in the yard and searched there. In the garden, too.

Edgar refilled his father's glass and said: Take your time,

don't drink so quickly. The driver got up and pissed in the ditch, said Edgar's father. He put his empty glass down on the table. What do you mean, take your time? he said. I'm in no hurry. The driver pissed into the ditch, said Edgar's father, and the ducks waddled over to watch him. They thought they were getting fresh water the way they do every afternoon. The driver laughed, buttoned up his fly, and broke off a piece of rotten wood from the bridge rail. He crushed it in his hand and scattered the chips in the grass. The ducks thought they were getting wheat the way they do every afternoon, and they gobbled up the rotten wood.

Since the search, the little wooden manikin has been missing from the bedside table, the little figure that Edgar's Brazilian uncle had carved when he was a boy.

Edgar's uncles were SS-men who hadn't come home. The lost war drove them in different directions. They had each made graveyards with the death's head brigades, and they parted at the end of the war. In their heads they carried the same baggage. They never sought one another out. Each helped himself to a local woman, and with her each built a steep roof, a pointed gable, four windows with grass-green windowframes, and a fence of grass-green posts, in Austria and in Brazil. They arrived in their foreign provinces and built two Swabian houses. As Swabian as their skulls, in two foreign places, where everything was different. And when their houses were finished, they made their wives two Swabian babies.

Only the trees in front of the houses, which they pruned every year the way they used to do at home before the war, outgrew the Swabian pattern, according to the different latitude, soil, and climate.

We sat in the scruffy park and ate Edgar's hazelnuts. Edgar said: They taste like gall. He had taken his shoe off and was smashing the nuts open with his heel. He laid the nuts out on a piece of newspaper. He didn't eat any himself. Georg gave me a key and sent me to the summerhouse for the first time.

I took the key out of my shoe. I unlocked the door. I didn't switch on the light, I lit a match. There was the pump, like a tall, thin man with one arm. An old jacket was hanging on its pipe. Underneath it was a rusty watering can. Propped against the wall were hoes, spades, rakes, pruning shears, a twig broom. There was soil on the tools. I lifted the lid of the well, the sack was dangling over a deep hole. I took it off its hook, put the books in it, and reattached it. I locked the door after me.

I crossed the same bit of grass I had trodden down when I came in. Mallows, made up entirely of purple thimbles, and mullein clutched at the air. Bindweed smelled sweet in the evening, or was it my fear? Each blade of grass pricked at my calves. Then a lost chick cheeped across the path and ran off as my shoes approached. The grass was three times its height and closed over its head. The chick lamented in this flowering wilderness, couldn't find a way out, ran for its life. The grasshoppers twittered, but the chick was much louder. It will give me away in its fear, I thought. Every plant kept its eye on me. My skin was throbbing from my scalp down to my belly.

There wasn't anyone in the summerhouse, I reported the following day. We were sitting in the bodega garden. The beer was green, because the bottles were green. Edgar, Kurt, and Georg had wiped the dust off the table with their bare arms. You could see on the surface where their arms had been. Behind their heads were the green leaves of the chestnut tree. The yellow ones were still hiding. We clinked glasses and didn't speak.

Across a forehead, on a temple, next to a cheek that belonged to Edgar, Kurt, or Georg, the hair became transparent because the sun was beating down on it. Or because the beer gurgled when one or the other of them set his bottle down on the table. Occasionally a yellow leaf fell from the tree. Then one or the other of us would turn up his eyes as though to see the leaf fall once again. We didn't wait for the next leaf, which fell a little later. Our eyes lacked the patience. We didn't commit ourselves to leaves. Only to flying splashes of yellow that distracted our faces from one another's.

The table was as hot as an iron. The skin tautened in our faces. High noon was burning down, the bodega was deserted. The workers were still making tin sheep and wooden melons in their factories. We ordered another round, so we could have more bottles between our arms.

Georg lowered his head, making a second chin under the first. He crooned to himself:

Yellow canary bird
yellow as yolk
with feathers so soft
and eyes so far away.

The song was very well known in our country. But two months earlier, the singers had fled over the border and the song was banned. Georg washed the song back down his throat with beer.

The waiter leaned against a tree trunk and listened and yawned. We weren't guests here; we looked at the waiter's grimy jacket and Edgar said: When it comes to children, fathers understand everything. My father understands why the men took away the wooden manikin. My father says: Their children like to play, too.

Edgar, Kurt, Georg, and I didn't want to leave the country. Not via the Danube, not through the air, not with the freight train. We went into the scruffy park. Edgar said: If only the right person would have to leave, everyone else would be able to stay in the country. He didn't believe it himself. Nobody believed that the right person would have to go. Every day we heard rumors about the old and new illnesses of the dictator. Nobody believed them, either. Even so, everyone whispered into the nearest ear. We too passed the rumors on, as if they contained the deadly, creeping virus that might finally catch up with the dictator: lung cancer, we whispered, throat cancer, bowel cancer, Alzheimer's, paralysis, leukemia.

He had to go away again, it was whispered: to France or China, Belgium or England, Korea, Libya, Syria, Germany or Cuba. In the whispers, each of his trips was coupled with our desire to flee.

Each flight was an offer, a bid for death. That's why the whispering had this undertow. Half the flights were cut short by the dogs and the bullets of the guards.

The flowing water, the moving freight trains, and the fields full of grain were all places of death. When the farmers harvested their cornfields, they found withered or bloated corpses, picked over by crows. The farmers took the corn and left the corpses, because it was better not to see them. In late autumn, the tractors ploughed them under.

Our fear of flight turned every one of the dictator's trips abroad into a medical crisis. The Far Eastern climate was to help against lung cancer, dwarf-elder roots against throat cancer, special battery belts against bowel cancer, acupuncture against Alzheimer's, baths against paralysis. There was only one sickness, it was said, that he didn't have to go abroad for: children's blood, to help against leukemia, he gets that here at home. In the maternity clinics it's pumped from the heads of newborn babies with Japanese vacuum syringes.

The rumors about the dictator's illnesses resembled the

letters that Edgar, Kurt, Georg, and I got from our mothers. The whispering warned us to hold off on flight. Everyone felt joy at the dictator's imminent demise, but no demise came. Everyone could feel the dictator's corpse, like his own wretched life, creeping through his skull. Everyone wanted to outlive him.

I went into the eating area and tore open the refrigerator. The light went on, as though I were beaming it in from outside.

Since Lola's death there had been no more tongues and livers in the fridge. But I could see them and smell them just the same. I could imagine to myself a transparent man standing by the open fridge. He was sick, and in order to live longer he had stolen the organ meats of healthy animals.

I could see his heart-beast. It was shut up in the electric bulb, coiled and tired. I slammed the fridge door shut, because the heart-beast hadn't been stolen. It had to be his, it was uglier than the organs of all the animals in the world.

The girls walked around inside the cube, laughed, and ate bread and grapes without turning on the light, although it was getting dark. Then someone switched the light on to get into bed. They all lay down. I turned off the light. The girls' breathing quickly settled into sleep. It was as though I could see it. As though their breathing, not the night, was black, still, and warm.

I lay uncovered and looked at the white linens on the beds. How do you have to live, I wondered, to be in harmony with what you honestly think? How do things manage—

objects lying in the street? How do they manage not to draw attention as you walk by—even though someone has lost them?

Then Father died. His liver got to be as big as that of a force-fed goose, from booze, said the doctor. Next to his face there were forceps and scissors in a glass case. I said: His liver is as big as his songs for the Führer. The doctor put his finger to his lips. He thought I meant songs for the dictator, but I meant the Führer. With his finger on his lips he said: A hopeless case. He meant Father, but I thought he meant the dictator.

Father was discharged from the hospital to die. He smiled out of the thinnest face he had ever had. He was so stupid he felt happy. The doctor's no good, he said, the room's bad, the bed's hard, and the pillows are stuffed with rags instead of feathers. That's why I've been going downhill, he said. The wristwatch slipped about on his wrist. His gums had shrivelled. He kept his dentures in his coat pocket because they no longer fitted his mouth.

Father was as withered as a beanpole. Only his liver had grown, his eyes, and his nose. And Father's nose was a beak, like that of a goose.

We're going to a different hospital, said Father. I carried his little valise. They have good doctors there, said Father.

On the street corner, the wind blew the hair into our faces and we looked at each other. Father took advantage of the opportunity and said: I have to go to the barber.

He was so stupid he was worrying about a haircut three

days before his death. We were both so stupid that he looked at his loose wristwatch and I nodded. That a couple of minutes later he was sitting and I was standing in the barber's shop. We were so untied from each other three days before his death that we could both watch as the barber in his white apron seized the hair in his scissors.

I carried Father's little valise into town. It contained a wristwatch, a set of dentures, and some brown-and-white-checked slippers. The undertaker had dressed Father in his street shoes. Everything that belongs to Father should be with him in his coffin, I thought to myself.

The brown-and-white-checked slippers have a brown cuff around the ankle. Where the two halves of the cuff meet are two brown-and-white-checked woolen tassels. The father has worn those slippers ever since the child was born. When he slips them on, his ankles become even bonier than when he's barefoot. When the father goes to sleep, the child is allowed to stroke the tassels with her hands. She is not allowed to step on them, though, not even in her bare feet.

The father sits on the edge of the bed, the child on the floor. The child hears the ticking of the clock and strokes the tassels in time with it. The mother is already asleep. As the child strokes the tassels, she says: Ticktock, ticktock. The father puts one foot on the other. The child's hand is caught in between. It hurts. The child holds her breath and says nothing.

When the father lifts his foot off her hand, it's crushed.

Leave me alone, he says, or else . . . Then he takes her crushed hand between his, and says: Or else nothing.

People say it only snows when a good person dies. That's not true.

It started to snow as I walked into town after Father's death, carrying his little valise in my hand. The flakes swayed drunkenly through the air like bits of rag. The snow didn't stick to the stones, the wrought-iron curlicues of the fences, the handles of the garden gates, or the lids of the letter boxes. Only in the hair of men and women did it stay white.

Instead of worrying about death, I thought, my father was doing something with the barber. He was doing something wrong with the first barber he found on the nearest street corner, just as he was doing something wrong with death. He didn't say a word about death to the barber. Even though Father felt he was dying, he was counting on staying alive.

I was so stupid that because of the ragged bits of snow falling white on the hair of men and women, I had to do something right with myself. I had to go with the little valise to my own hairdresser a day before my father's funeral and tell him something about death.

I stayed with my hairdresser as long as I could and told him everything I knew about my father's life.

In this tale of death, my father's life began at a time I knew best from the books of Edgar, Kurt, and Georg and least from Father himself: An SS-man who came back from the war, who had made graveyards and left places in a hurry,

I told the hairdresser. Someone who had had to make a child and always keep an eye on his slippers. As I talked about his damn stupid plants, his dark, dark plums, his boozy songs for the Führer, and his swollen liver, I was getting a permanent wave for his funeral.

Before I left, the hairdresser said: My father was at Stalingrad.

I boarded the train and rode to Father's funeral and Mother's back-pains. The fields were brown-and-white-checked.

I stood by the coffin. My singing grandmother came into the room with a quilt. She walked around the coffin and laid the quilt on the burial shroud. Her nose looked like his beak. He's making the most of it, I thought, getting her to look after him. Her lips pouted into a hoarse, lonely whistle as she sang to herself, her reason gone. It was years since my singing grandmother had recognized anyone in the house. Now she recognized Father, because she was crazy and he was dead. Now his heart-beast was lodged in her.

She said to Mother: Leave the quilt on the coffin, the snow goose is coming. Mother pressed one hand against her bad back and, with the other, tore the quilt off the burial shroud.

Ever since the searches, Edgar, Kurt, and Georg carried toothbrushes and hand towels in their jacket pockets. They were expecting to be arrested.

To see if anyone in their rooms was tampering with their suitcases, they laid two hairs on the lid each morning. By evening, the hairs would be gone.

Kurt said: Every evening, when I go to bed I can feel these cold hands under my back. I turn on my side and draw up my legs. The thought of going to sleep is horrifying. I fall asleep as quickly as a stone dropping into water.

Edgar said: I dreamed I was going to the movies. I had just shaved, because there was a sign in the glass display case by the entrance saying you could only leave the dormitory if you had just shaved. I went to the tram stop. On every seat in the streetcar lay a piece of paper with the days of the week on it. I read: Monday, Tuesday, Wednesday, all the days up to Sunday. I said to the conductor: Today isn't one of those days. The conductor said: That's why everyone has to stand. Everyone was standing crowded together near the rear exit. Each was carrying a baby in his arms. The babies were singing in chorus. They sang together even though they couldn't see each other past the grown-ups.

The cubes of Edgar, Kurt, and Georg and the houses of their parents were searched three more times. After each search, their mothers wrote them letters full of their illnesses. Edgar's father didn't visit the city again, his mother's letter came in the mail. Edgar's father wrote in the margin: You are driving your mother to an early grave.

My room was searched too. When I walked in, the girls were just cleaning up. My bedding, the mattress, and the soot for my eyelashes were all on the floor. My suitcase was by the window wide open, with my patent stockings in the lid. On the stockings lay a letter from my mother.

Someone screamed: You drove Lola to her death. I tore open the letter, kicked the suitcase shut, and said: You're mistaking me for the gym teacher. Someone said very quietly: I don't think so. Lola hanged herself with your belt. I picked up my eyelash soot and flung it across the room. It hit the preserving jar with pine twigs in it that was on the table. The tips of the twigs were leaning against the wall.

I read the letter. Behind my mother's back-pains was written:

Three men arrived in a car. Two of them made a huge mess in the house. The third was just the driver. He talked to Grandmother so she'd leave the other two in peace. The driver speaks German, he even has a Swabian accent like us. He comes from one of the neighboring villages, he didn't want to say which one. Grandmother mistook him for your father, she wanted to comb his hair. He took the comb away from her, then she started singing. He was struck by how beautifully she sang. He even joined in on one song:

Home now, children, for the night
Mama's blowing out the light.

He said the tune he knew was a bit different. His version was pretty close to Grandmother's except he sang off-key.

Ever since the men went away, Grandfather hasn't had any peace. His white queen has disappeared. He's looked for her everywhere and can't find her. He misses her badly. He can't play chess unless he can find her. He took such good care of the pieces. They survived the war and his imprisonment. And now he loses the queen in his own home.

Grandfather says I'm to write you that other people manage to clap along with everyone else and make money. Don't do this to your grandfather again.

It was snowing. What fell on our faces as snow was already water when it hit the asphalt. Our feet were cold. The evening lifted the wet sheen of the street into the trees. The lamps wanted to swim together among the bare branches.

At the fountain, in the reflection, the man with the black bow tie was standing underneath himself once again. He looked up the prison street. The snow lingered on his withered bouquet just as it did in his hair. It was late, the buses with their prisoners had long since driven back to the prison.

The wind scattered snow in our faces, even though Edgar, Kurt, Georg, and I were going in the opposite direction. We wanted to go somewhere warm. But the bodega was too full of racket. We went into the movie theater for the last show. The film had already started.

A factory floor was buzzing on the screen. Once we had gotten used to the darkness, Edgar counted the shadows in the seats. Apart from us, there were nine people in the theater. We sat down in the back row. Kurt said: We can talk here.

The factory on the screen was dark, so we couldn't see each other. Edgar laughed and said: We all know what we look like anyway. Georg said: There are some that don't. He took his toothbrush out of his coat pocket and stuck it in his mouth. On the screen, the proletariat was running through the factory with iron bars in their hands, stoking a blast furnace. The molten iron lit up the theater. We looked at each other's faces and laughed. Kurt said: Take that toothbrush out of your mouth. Georg put it in his pocket. You Swabian fartfiddle, he said.

Kurt said: I dreamed I was at our barber's. All the other customers were women, knitting. I asked: What are they doing here? The barber said: They're waiting for their husbands. He shook my hand and said: We've never met. I thought he was referring to the women, but he was looking at me. I said: Of course we have. The women tittered. I'm the student, I said. First I've heard of it, said the barber. On second thought, I know someone who reminds me of you. But I don't know you.

The people in the theater were whistling and shouting: Go on, Lupu, fuck her, fuck her, give it to her. Two workers, a man and a woman, were kissing by the factory gate. The night wind was blowing. In the next shot it was day by the factory gate, and the kissed woman had a baby.

When I wanted to sit down in front of the mirror, said Kurt, the barber shook his head and said: Can't do that. I said: What do you mean? He tapped on the mirror with his finger. I looked at my reflection: there was pubic hair all over my face.

Georg plucked at my arm and put the key to the summerhouse in my hand. Where am I supposed to keep it? I asked.

On the screen, children were running out of the school gates onto the street. The child of the kissed woman worker

70

was met outside the school by its father, Lupu. He gave the child a kiss on the forehead and relieved him of his schoolbag.

Georg said: I got bad grades in school. My father said: It's time we sewed something for the headmaster, the best thing would be a pair of trousers. The next day my mother went out and bought some gray cloth, hemming tape, canvas for the pockets, and buttons for the fly, because the only zippers they had in the shop were red. My father came to school and invited the headmaster to come have his measurements taken. He'd been waiting for this offer for a long time, and he went along right away.

The headmaster stood next to the sewing machine. My mother started measuring down by his ankles. Keep your legs quite relaxed, Mr. Headmaster, she said. How long? she asked. Let it out a little. How wide? Take it in a little. Would you like cuffs, Mr. Headmaster? She asked her way up the trousers he had on. How about pockets, Mr. Headmaster? At the crotch, she took a deep breath and asked: And where do you carry the key to the cellar, Mr. Headmaster, on the left or the right? Always on the right, he said. And for the cellar door, she asked, would you rather have buttons or a zipper? What do you advise? the headmaster asked. A zipper is more practical, but buttons have more character, my father said. Buttons then, said the headmaster.

After the theater, I went to my seamstress. Her children were already asleep. We stayed in the kitchen. It was the first

71

time I had been to see her so late. She wasn't surprised. We ate baked apples. She smoked, sucked in her cheeks, and her face looked like one of Grandfather's chess queens. The bastard's in Canada now, she said, I bumped into his sister today. The seamstress's husband had fled by taking the Danube, without saying a word to her. I had told her about the light and dark queens and Grandfather's company barber and about my singing and praying grandmothers. And about Father's damn stupid plants, and Mother's backpains.

Your two grandmothers remind me of your grandfather's two chess queens, she had said. The praying one is the dark queen, and the singing one is light. Praying is always dark.

I didn't contradict her, but for me it was the other way around.

My singing grandmother is the dark one. She knows that everyone has a heart-beast. She steals another woman's husband. He loves the other woman, he doesn't love my singing grandmother. But she gets him because she wants him. Or not him so much as his field. And she keeps him. He doesn't love her, but she can control him by saying: Your heart-beast is a mouse.

Then everything turned out to be for nothing, because the field was expropriated by the government after the war.

The shock of that caused my grandmother to start singing.

The seamstress never realized how little she knew about me. It seemed to be enough for her that I was a student and never wore a belt.

I laid the key to the summerhouse on the seamstress's windowsill and left it there. I thought to myself: No one would throw away a key.

Edgar, Kurt, and Georg all thought the seamstress was unreliable. I said: You're only suspicious because your mothers are seamstresses. I had to promise not to involve the seamstress in anything that concerned us. Edgar, Kurt, and Georg wouldn't have agreed to my leaving the key on the windowsill. They would have recited the following poem, as they so often did when they felt suspicious:

Everyone had a friend in every wisp of cloud
that's how it is with friends where the world is full of fear
even my mother said, that's how it is
friends are out of the question
think of more serious things.

Late that night I walked back to the dormitory. I met three guards on the way, but they didn't bother me. They were preoccupied, eating green plums as if it were daytime.

It was so quiet in the city, I could hear them chewing. I stepped softly so as not to disturb them as they ate. Ideally I would have walked on tiptoe, but that would have attracted their attention. I made myself as light as a shadow as I walked; no one could have taken hold of me. I walked neither too fast nor too slow. The green plums in the guards' hands were as black as night.

Two weeks later, I went to the seamstress's in the early afternoon. Right away she said: You forgot your key, I found it the next day. All day long I thought about it being night and you being locked out of your dormitory.

The tape measure hung round the seamstress's neck. It's not the dormitory key, I said, it's from home. And I thought to myself: She wears the tape measure like a belt around her neck.

Then the tea boiled in the kettle. She said: I watch my children growing up, and I hope later on they'll want to use the key to their home more often than you do. She spilled sugar near my cup. Can you understand that? she asked. I nodded.

Because we were afraid, Edgar, Kurt, Georg, and I met every day. We sat together at a table, but our fear stayed locked within each of our heads, just as we'd brought it to our meetings. We laughed a lot, to hide it from each other. But fear always finds an out. If you control your face, it slips into your voice. If you manage to keep a grip on your face and your voice, as if they were dead wood, it will slip out through your fingers. It will pass through your skin and lie there. You can see it lying around on objects close by.

We could see whose fear was where, because we had known each other so long. Often we couldn't stand each other, because we were all we had. We had no choice but to lash out at each other.

You and your Swabian forgetfulness. You and your Swabian impatience, or your Swabian lolling about. You and your Swabian penny-pinching. You and your Swabian clumsiness. You and your Swabian hiccups, or sneezing; you and your Swabian socks, or shirts, we said.

You Swabian farthorn, you Swabian cabbagehead, you Swabian ragbag. We needed the rage from all those words to separate us. We invented them like curses to gain distance from one another. Our laughter was hard, we used it to drill into our pain. Everything happened quickly, because we knew each other inside out. We knew exactly how to hurt each other, and we enjoyed watching each other suffer. Watching each other collapse under our rough love and realizing how little we could endure. One insult led to the next like beads on a string until the victim stopped speaking. And stayed that way for some time. And for some time after that, words would fall upon his silent countenance like locusts on a field already chewed bare.

In our fear, we had seen more deeply into one another than was allowed. In our long trust, we needed the change of pace. Hate was allowed to trample and destroy. To mow the love that sprang up in our closeness like long grass. Apologies took back the insult in no more time than you can hold your breath.

We always picked our quarrels deliberately; only their consequences were inadvertent. Each time the rage subsided, we declared our mutual love without inventing any words. Our love was always there. But in our quarrels, it grew claws.

Once Edgar said, as he handed me the keys to the summerhouse: You and your Swabian smile. I felt the claws, and don't know how my mouth didn't drop out of my face. As I automatically felt around for a reply, I felt so abandoned that I couldn't think of a word to say for myself. Maybe my mouth was a ripe peapod. That's how tight and withered I imagined the lips I wished weren't mine. A Swabian smile was like my father, whom I hadn't been able to choose. Like my mother, whom I didn't want.

Another time we were in the movie theater, in the back row. That time too there was a factory floor on the screen. A woman worker was spooling woolen yarn into a knitting machine. Another woman came along with a red apple and watched. The first woman smoothed out the yarn in the machine and said: I think I'm in love. She took the other woman's apple and bit into it.

During that film, Kurt laid his hand on my arm. That time too he told me a dream. In this dream, there were men at the barber's. Up on the wall was a slate with a crossword puzzle on it. All the men pointed coat hangers at the empty squares and suggested letters. The barber stood on a ladder and wrote them in. Kurt sat down in front of the mirror. The men said: There'll be no haircuts until we've solved the puzzle. We were here first. When Kurt got up to leave, the barber called after him: Make sure you bring along your razor tomorrow.

What am I doing dreaming about a razor? Kurt asked in my ear, even though he knew the reason. Edgar, Kurt, and Georg no longer had any razors. They had disappeared out of their locked suitcases.

I had stayed at the river too long with Edgar, Kurt, and Georg. Let's take another stroll, they said, as if we'd been enjoying a carefree walk along the river. We still knew how to walk slowly or quickly, we could still sneak or pursue. But strolling was something we had forgotten how to do.

Mother wants to pick the last of the plums in the garden. But the ladder has a loose rung. Grandfather goes out to buy nails. Mother waits under the tree. She's wearing her apron with the deepest pockets. It gets dark.

When Grandfather takes the chess pieces out of his jacket and sets them up on the table, my singing grandmother says: The plums are waiting, and you're going to play chess with the barber. Grandfather says: The barber wasn't home, so I went out into the field. I'll go get the nails tomorrow, today I was just lollygagging about.

Kurt turned his toes in as he walked, he threw a stick in the water and said:

Everyone had a friend in every wisp of cloud
that's how it is with friends where the world is full of fear
even my mother said, that's how it is
friends are out of the question
think of more serious things.

Edgar, Kurt, and Georg were forever reciting that poem. In the bodega, in the scruffy park, in the tram, in the movie theater. Even on the way to the barber's.

Edgar, Kurt, and Georg often went to the barber's together. When they walked in the door the barber said: All right, one at a time please, two red and one black. Kurt and Georg always got their hair cut ahead of Edgar.

The poem came from one of the books in the summerhouse. I could say it by heart too. But only to myself, to have something to hold on to when I had to be with the girls in the cube. I was too ashamed to say the poem in front of Edgar, Kurt, and Georg.

I tried it once in the scruffy park and got stuck after the second line. Edgar rattled off the rest, and I picked a worm off the wet ground, pulled Edgar's collar open at the back, and dropped the cold red worm down his shirt.

There was always a wisp of cloud in the city, or else just an empty sky. And the letters from my mother, or yours, or his, that had nothing to say. The poem hid its chilly laughter. That went well with the voices of Edgar, Kurt, and Georg. It was easy to recite. But to keep up that chilly laughter day after day was hard. Maybe that's why it had to be recited so often.

Don't be taken in by false friendliness, Edgar, Kurt, and

Georg warned me. The girls in the room will try everything, they said, just like the boys in our room. When they ask you when you're coming back, what they mean is: How long will you be gone?

Captain Pjele, who had the same name as his dog, first interrogated Edgar, Kurt, and Georg about this poem.

Captain Pjele had the text of the poem on a piece of paper. He crumpled it up; Pjele the dog barked. Kurt was made to open his mouth, and the captain stuffed the piece of paper into it. Kurt had to eat the poem. It made him gag. Pjele the dog jumped at him twice, tore his trousers, and scratched his legs. The third time, Kurt reckoned, the dog Pjele would certainly have bitten him. But Captain Pjele said in a quiet, bored voice: That's enough, Pjele. Captain Pjele complained about his kidneys and said: You're lucky you've got me.

Edgar had to stand in a corner of the room for an hour without moving. The dog Pjele sat in front of him and watched. His tongue hung out of his mouth. I thought, I'll kick him in the snout so hard he won't pick himself up, said Edgar. The dog sensed what was going through my mind. Each time Edgar moved so much as a finger or took a slightly deeper breath to keep from having to shift his weight, Pjele the dog growled. At the slightest move he would have leapt, said Edgar. I wouldn't have survived that, I wouldn't have had the self-control. There would have been a bloodbath.

Before Edgar was allowed to leave, Captain Pjele complained about his kidneys and the dog Pjele licked Edgar's shoes. Captain Pjele said: You're lucky you've got me.

Georg had to lie on his belly, with his hands behind his back. The dog Pjele sniffed at his neck and temples. Then he licked his hands. Georg didn't know how long that went on. A pot of cyclamen stood on Captain Pjele's desk, said Georg. When Georg came in the door, the cyclamen had only one blossom open. When he was allowed to go, it had two. Captain Pjele complained about his kidneys and said: You're lucky you've got me.

Captain Pjele said to Edgar, Kurt, and Georg that the poem was an incitement to flee the country. They said: It's an old folk song. Captain Pjele said: It would be better for your sake if one of you had written it. That would be bad enough, but not as bad as this. Maybe it was a folk song once, but those were different times. The rule of the bourgeoisie and the landowning class is long gone. Today our people sing different songs.

Edgar, Kurt, Georg, and I walked along the river bank, following the trees and the drift of our conversation. Edgar had returned the key of the summerhouse to the man above suspicion. We had divided the books, photographs, and notebooks among ourselves.

Breath from each of our mouths crept into the chill air. In front of our faces was a herd of fleeing beasts. I said to Georg: Look, your heart-beast is moving on.

Georg put his thumb under my chin: You and your Swabian heart-beast, he laughed. Drops of spittle flew in my face. I lowered my eyes and saw Georg's fingers by my chin. His knuckles were white, and his fingers blue with cold. I wiped the spit from my face. Lola had called the spit in the lash-soot "monkey grease." "And you're solid wood through and through," I snapped back.

Our heart-beasts fled like mice. They sloughed off their skins and disappeared into nothingness. When we spoke in rapid succession, they hung in the air a little longer.

When you write, don't forget to put the date, and always put a hair with the letter, said Edgar. If there isn't one, we'll know the letter's been opened.

Single hairs, I thought to myself, crisscrossing the country on trains. A dark hair of Edgar's, a light one of mine. A red one of Kurt or of Georg. They were both called Goldilocks by the students. The word nail-clippers in a sentence will mean interrogation, said Kurt, shoes will mean a search, a sentence about having a cold will mean you're being followed. After the greeting always an exclamation point, but a comma if your life's in danger.

The trees on the riverbank drooped into the water. There were pollarded willows and crack willows. When I was little, the names of plants used to give me reasons for what I did. But these trees didn't know why Edgar, Kurt, Georg, and I were walking by the river. Everything around us smelled of farewell. None of us said the word.

A child is afraid of dying and eats even more green plums and doesn't know why. She stands in the garden and asks the plants. But the plants, the leaves and the stalks, don't understand why the girl is using her hands and her mouth against her own life. Only the names of the plants know why: trefoil, cotton grass, milk thistle, crowfoot, cinquefoil, viper's grass, shepherd's club, black alder, thorn apple, monkshood.

I was the last to leave the cube in the dormitory. The girls' beds were all stripped when I came back from the river. Their suitcases were gone; in the closet, only my clothes still hung. The loudspeaker was silent. I stripped the bed. Without a pillow in it, the pillowcase was a sack for a head. I folded it up. I put the box of lash-soot in my coat pocket. Without a blanket in it, the blanket cover was a bodybag. I folded it up.

When I picked up the blanket to pull off the cover, I found a pig's ear in the middle of the sheet. That was the girls' way of saying farewell. I shook the sheet but the ear didn't move, it was sewn on in the middle like a button. I could see where the needle had pierced the bluish cartilage, and the black thread. I wasn't able to feel disgust. More than of the pig's ear, I was afraid of the closet. I took all my clothes out in one armful and dropped them in the suitcase. Eye shadow, eye pencil, powder, and lipstick were all in the suitcase.

What were four years anyway? Did they show on me or on the clothes? The last year was hanging in the closet. I had put on makeup every morning this past year. The less I wanted to live, the more I wanted to make up.

I folded the sheet up, ear and all.

At the end of the corridor lay a pile of bedding. In front of it stood a woman in a pale blue overall. She was counting pillowcases. When I gave her my bedding, she stopped counting. She scratched herself with a pencil, I said my name. She took a list out of her overall pocket, looked through it, and made a cross. She said: You're the second-to-last. The last, I said; the second-to-last is dead.

On that day, Lola in her nylons might have boarded a train. And the following day someone bringing the sheep home through the snow might have expected his sister to step out of the train, barefoot in the cold.

I must have stood once more in front of the empty closet before I carried my suitcase out of the cube. Moments earlier I had once more opened the window. The clouds in the sky were like specks of snow on a ploughed field. The winter sun had teeth. I saw my face in the window and waited for the sun to withdraw its light from the city, since it had enough earth and snow where it was, in the sky.

When I went out onto the street with my suitcase, I felt I ought to turn back and shut the closet door. The window was left open. The closet, perhaps, was shut.

I took a tram to the station and boarded the train that carried Mother's letters. Four hours later I was home. The grandfather clock had stopped, the alarm clock had stopped. Mother had put on her Sunday best, or so it seemed to me, because I hadn't seen her for a long time. She put out her index finger to run it over my whisper-thin nylons, and then pulled it back. She said: My hands are so rough, so now you're a translator. On her wrist was Father's wristwatch. The wristwatch had stopped as well.

Since Father's death, Mother had overwound all the clocks in the house. The springs were shot. When I wind them, she said, I think maybe I ought to stop, but then I go on.

Grandfather put his chess pieces out on the board. I have to imagine the queens, he said. I've told you before you ought to carve yourself some new ones, said Mother. We have enough wood. Grandfather said: I don't feel like it.

My singing grandmother walked around my suitcase. She looked me in the face and said: Who's this? Mother said: You know who it is. My singing grandmother asked: Where's your husband? I said: I don't have one. My singing grandmother asked: Does he wear a hat?

Edgar had moved far away to a grimy industrial city. Everyone in the city made tin sheep and called it metallurgy.

I visited Edgar in late summer. I saw the thick chimneys, the clouds of red smoke, and the slogans. The bodega with cloudy mulberry schnapps and the reeling home to the bare blocks of tenements. The old people hobbling through the grass. The tiniest ragged children eating mallow seeds by the roadside. Their little arms couldn't reach up to the mulberry branches yet. The old people called the mallow seeds manna. They said it made you wise. The scraggy dogs and cats were quite undisturbed by us as they hunted and pounced on mice and beetles.

When the sun is hot in midsummer, said Edgar, all the

cats and dogs lie under the mulberry trees and sleep. When the sun warms their fur, they get too weak to do anything about their hunger. The pigs in the withered grass eat the fermenting mulberries and keel over. They're as drunk as the people.

When winter came, the pigs were slaughtered between the high-rise apartment blocks. If it doesn't snow much, the grass stays bloody all winter, said Edgar.

Edgar and I walked over to the dilapidated school. The sun flashed; wherever it happened to shine there were flies. They were small, but not dull-gray and sluggish like flies that had hatched too late in the year. These were metallic-green, and they buzzed as they settled on my hair. They let themselves be carried for a few steps, and then they buzzed away again, into the air.

In the summer, they settle on sleeping beasts, said Edgar. They let themselves rise and fall to the rhythms of the breathing beneath the pelt.

Edgar was a teacher in the city. Four hundred pupils, the youngest are six, the oldest ten, said Edgar. They eat mulberries to keep their voice in shape for the Party songs and they eat manna so that they can be wise and remember their multiplication tables. They play soccer to improve their leg muscles and practise handwriting for dexterity. Their insides suffer from diarrhea, and their outsides from scrapes and lice.

Horsedrawn wagons moved more quickly about the city streets than the buses. The wagon wheels clattered, the hooves made a dull ringing sound. Here the horses didn't wear high heels, instead they had red and green woolen tassels dangling in front of their eyes. The same tassels were on the whips. The horses are beaten so hard that the tassels from the whips became imprinted on their memories, said Edgar. Then the same tassels are dangled in front of their eyes. The horses trot on out of fear.

Edgar said: The buses are full of people sitting with their heads down. You'd think they were asleep. My first few days I couldn't understand how they managed to wake up at the right stop. But if you go on a bus, you'll put your head down in the same way. The floors are gone. You can see the road through the holes.

I saw this city reflected in Edgar's face, smack in the middle of his eyes, at the edges of his cheeks, and around his mouth. His hair was long, his face in the middle of it looked to me like a bare place that shunned the light. His veins were showing through his temples, his eyes twitched for no reason, the lids fell over them. The eyes darted away if you so much as glanced into them.

Edgar shared an apartment with a gym instructor, two rooms, one kitchen and one bathroom. Mulberry trees and tall burdocks stood outside the windows. Every day a rat came up through the plughole in the bath. The gym instructor has kept it in the house for years, said Edgar, he leaves bits of bacon for it in the tub. He calls it Emil. It also eats mulberries and young burdocks.

I could see Lola's province in Edgar's face. I wanted to be rid of my fear for Edgar. My fear imagined it was impossible to stick it out here for three years. But Edgar had to stay here for three years. He had been sent here as a teacher by the state. And so I didn't say anything about the place. But late in the evening, when we looked through his window at the half-moon, Edgar said: Everywhere you look you see Lola's notebook. It's as big as the sky.

The closet in Edgar's room was empty. His clothes lay in his suitcase so that he could leave the place anytime without having to pack. I won't make myself at home here, said Edgar. I noticed two hairs lying crosswise on the lid of the suitcase. Edgar said: The gym instructor noses around in my room.

On the way to the dilapidated school I wanted to pick some burdocks, because Edgar had an empty vase, and the late shoots were still blooming. I bent them and tugged at them, but I couldn't manage to break any off. I left them by the wayside, bent in half. Their stalks had fibers of steel. The prickly seeds of the dead burdocks I hadn't wanted to pick clung to my coat.

The children make themselves epaulettes out of those burrs, said Edgar. They want to be officers and policemen when they grow up. The chimneys carry them off into the factories. Only a very few, the toughest among them, still cling to life by the skin of their teeth. Like the burdocks that leapt onto your coat, said Edgar, they will jump onto trains and become guards, ready for anything, standing by the wayside somewhere in the country.

Georg had been sent off for three years to teach in an industrial town where everyone made wooden melons. The wooden melons were called wood-processing industry.

Edgar had been to see Georg. His town was in the middle of the forest. No trains or buses went there. Only trucks with monosyllabic drivers, all missing a few fingers, Edgar had said. The trucks arrive empty and leave loaded with tree trunks.

The workers steal scraps of wood and make them into parquet floors at home, Georg had told Edgar. Anyone who doesn't steal isn't taken seriously at the factory. And so, even if their apartments have wall-to-wall parquet, they can't stop stealing and laying more. The parquet eventually covers the walls, right up to the ceiling.

Two sawmills hissed away in the middle of the town. At the far ends of the streets you could hear axes chopping in the forest. And every so often you could hear, somewhere behind the town, the crash of a heavy tree falling to the ground. All the men on the streets have fingers missing, Edgar had said, and the children, too.

When the first letter from Georg reached me, the date on the envelope was two weeks old. The same date as on Edgar's letter, which had arrived three days earlier.

I opened Georg's letter just as slowly as I'd opened Edgar's three days before. There was a red hair in the fold of the stationery. Three days before there had been a black one in Edgar's letter. After the greeting was an exclamation mark. I gulped as I read and moved my lips, lest there be any sentences with a cold, nail-scissors, or shoes in them. The gulping didn't help. Those sentences came. They had come in Edgar's letter, too.

The people here have sawdust in their hair and in their eyebrows, wrote Georg.

The words in our mouths do as much damage as our feet on the grass, I thought to myself. I thought of the last walk with Edgar, Kurt, and Georg by the river. Of Georg's spit on my cheek, his fingers under my chin. I heard myself say to Georg: You're solid wood, through and through.

That sentence wasn't mine. It really didn't have anything to do with wood. Then. I had often heard it said by others, if someone treated them roughly. It wasn't their sentence either. If someone treated them roughly, they thought of it because they too had often heard it from others who were treated roughly. If the sentence had ever had anything to do with wood, it would have been important to discover whose it was. But it only had to do with roughness. When the roughness was over, so was the sentence.

Months had passed, but the sentence hadn't passed. It seemed to me that my words had predicted Georg's fate: You're solid wood through and through.

My red hair doesn't attract attention here, because it looks as though it's got sawdust in it, he said in the letter. I walk aimlessly through the town. In front of me is someone else, walking aimlessly. If we're going far, we fall into step. Here, you keep four full paces' distance, so as not to bother each other. Whoever's in front makes sure my steps don't get too near. And, behind, I make sure their backs don't get too close to me.

But on two occasions already, it has turned out differently. The man in front of me suddenly put both his hands in his trouser pockets. He stopped and turned his pockets inside out, to shake the sawdust out of them. He patted the sawdust out of his pockets, and I overtook him. Shortly afterward, I heard him more than four paces behind me, then just four. And then breathing down my neck. He overtook me and started running. Once he ran out of sawdust, he was no longer aimless.

The old men cut off young branches, saw them into lengths, hollow them out, and make little holes in them. The front end is squared off like a mouthpiece. Each branch they touch, wrote Georg, they make into a whistle.

There are whistles no longer than a baby's finger, Edgar had said, and whistles as big as a full-grown man.

The old men go into the forest with their whistles and drive the birds crazy. The birds lose their way among the trees and nests. And once they get outside the forest, they mistake the water in the puddles for the sky. They plummet to their deaths.

There is only one bird here who has his own life, wrote Georg; it's called the ninekiller shrike, or butcher bird. Its voice is unlike any whistle. It drives the old men crazy. They cut branches of buckthorn, and bloody their fingers on the thorns. They make finger-width, child-size, whistles from its wood, but the butcher bird refuses to go crazy.

Edgar had said that when the butcher bird has eaten its fill, it goes on hunting. The old men creep around the buckthorn and whistle. The bird flies over their heads into the thicket and perches. It's quite imperturbable. It calmly spikes its prey on the thorns, against the next day's hunger.

That's the way to be, wrote Georg. I'm like that too, I bought myself two pairs of shoes in one week.

In Edgar's letter, three days before, I'd read: Twice already this week I couldn't find my shoes.

Whenever I walked past a shoestore, I thought of searches. I hurried by. The seamstress said: Children's shoes are so expensive. To hear her talk of shoes, meaning shoes, made me laugh. She said: You're all right, you don't have any children. I was thinking of something else, I said.

Kurt came into the city every week. He was working as an engineer in a slaughterhouse. It was located on the edge of a village not far from the city. There's really no reason to live in the village, with the city so near, said Kurt. But the buses go the wrong way. In the morning, when I need to go to work in the village, a bus leaves the village for the city. In the afternoon, after work, a bus goes from the city to the village. It's done deliberately, they don't want people who work in the slaughterhouse to go back to the city every day. They just want village people who live in the village. And if new people come in, they quickly turn them into accomplices. All it takes is a couple of days for them to get like the others, mute and addicted to drinking warm blood.

Kurt was in charge of a dozen workers. They were laying heating pipes in the slaughterhouse grounds. Kurt had had a cold for three weeks. Every week I said: You should stay in bed. The workers are just as stuffed-up as I am, and they don't stay in bed, he said. If I'm not there, they won't work, they'll just steal everything.

We didn't use the word cold, because that was for the letters. In our half hour together, Kurt drank three cups of tea to my one. I looked into my cup and thought: He drinks three times as much as I do, and he slurps. Then he said: The children at Georg's school want nothing to do with the factory and their parents' parquet and their grandparents' whistles. They whittle themselves guns and revolvers out of boards. They want to be policemen and officers.

When I go to the slaughterhouse in the morning, the children in the village are just on their way to school, said Kurt. They don't have books or notebooks, just a piece of chalk. With that they fill the walls and fences with hearts. Nothing but hearts, intertwined hearts. Pigs' and bulls' hearts, what else? The children are already accomplices. When their fathers kiss them goodnight, they smell the blood on their breath and they can't wait to go to the slaughterhouse themselves.

I had written to Edgar: I've had a cold for a week, and I can't find my nail-clippers.

To Georg I had written: I've had a cold for a week, and my nail-clippers don't cut.

Maybe I shouldn't have written cold and nail-clippers in the same sentence, maybe I should have put them in different parts of the letter. Maybe I should have written nail-clippers first and cold later on. But cold and nail-clippers had become like a pounding that was bigger than my head, after I'd spent the whole afternoon saying sentences to myself that had cold and nail-clippers in them, trying to find the right one.

Cold and nail-clippers had thrown me out of their own and our agreed-upon meanings. I could no longer see anything in them, and I left them standing inside a sentence that was possibly good and certainly bad. To cross out cold or nail-clippers in that one sentence only to write them again a few lines further on would have been still worse. In those two letters, I could have easily crossed out any other sentence. But to cross out cold and nail-clippers would have been a clue, and more stupid than a bad sentence.

I needed two hairs to put in my letters. In the mirror my hair was a long way from me and still within easy reach, like the pelt of a beast that a hunter observes through binoculars.

I had to tear out two hairs that wouldn't get lost, two true letter-hairs. Where were they growing, over my forehead, by the right or left temple, or on the crown of my head?

I ran a comb through my hair, hairs caught in the comb. I put one in the letter to Edgar and one in the letter to Georg. If they turned out not to be true letter-hairs, then it was the fault of the comb.

At the post office I licked the stamps. At the entrance there was a man telephoning, who followed me every day. He carried a white canvas bag and held a dog on a leash. The bag looked light, although it was half full. He carried it because he couldn't be sure where I was going.

I went into a shop. He joined the line a little later; he had to tie up his dog first. There were four women standing between him and me. When I left the shop, he set off after me again with the dog. The bag was no fuller than before.

While he was telephoning, he had held the leash and the

telephone in one hand and the bag in the other. He talked and watched as my tongue wet the stamps. I stuck the stamps on the envelopes, even though the corners weren't wet. I dropped the letters in the mailbox before his eyes, as though they'd be safe from him there.

The man was not Captain Pjele. The dog might be Pjele. But Captain Pjele wasn't the only one with a wolfhound.

I had been interrogated by Captain Pjele on his own without the dog Pjele. Maybe the dog Pjele was having a break, to eat or sleep. Maybe the dog Pjele was off in one of the building's many hidden rooms being trained, either learning something new or practicing something he already knew, while Captain Pjele was interrogating me. Maybe the dog Pjele was with the man and the canvas bag, on the tail of someone else in the street. Maybe with a different man and no canvas bag. Maybe the dog Pjele was following Kurt while Captain Pjele was interrogating me. How many men were there, and how many dogs? As many as a dog has hairs.

There was a piece of paper on the table. Captain Pjele said: Read. On the piece of paper was the poem. Read it out loud, so we can both enjoy it, said Captain Pjele. I read out:

Everyone had a friend in every wisp of cloud
that's how it is with friends where the world is full of fear

even my mother said, that's how it is
friends are out of the question
think of more serious things.

Captain Pjele asked: Who wrote that? I said: Nobody, it's a folk song. In that case it's the property of the people, said Captain Pjele, and therefore the people can carry on making songs and writing poems. Yes, I said. Then make up a poem, said Captain Pjele. I said: I can't. Well, I can, said Captain Pjele. I'll make up a poem and you write it down, that way we can both enjoy it:

I had three friends in every wisp of cloud
that's how it is with whores where the world is full of clouds
even my mother said, that's how it is
friends are out of the question
think of more serious things.

I had to sing Captain Pjele's words. I sang without hearing my voice. I fell from a fear full of doubt into a fear full of absolute certainty. I could sing the way water sings. Maybe the tune came from my singing grandmother's dementia. Perhaps I knew tunes she had lost with her reason. Perhaps things that lay fallow in her brain had to pass my lips.

Grandfather's barber is the same age as Grandfather. He's been a widower for years and years, even though his Anna was no older than my mother. For a long time he found it hard to come to terms with the death of his Anna.

When Anna was still alive, my mother said: She's got a loose tongue. When Grandfather's field was expropriated by the state, Anna had said to my singing grandmother: Now you've got what you deserve.

When the swastika flag was flying over the village sports field, my singing grandmother had denounced Anna's fiancé to the local Gruppenführer. She had said: Anna's fiancé never comes to the flag raising, because he doesn't like the Führer.

Two days later, a car came from the city and took Anna's fiancé away. He was never seen again.

When the war was long over, my mother said, the barber got young Anna. Even today the barber thanks Grandmother for getting him a wife as pretty as a picture. When he cuts Grandfather's hair or plays chess with him, he says: Women as pretty as a picture never get old, they die before they can get ugly.

But there's really no cause to be grateful, said Mother. Grandmother didn't want anything bad for Anna or anything good for the barber. She merely reported the fiancé because he hadn't wanted to join the army, while her own son had long been at war.

Captain Pjele took the piece of paper and said: What a pretty poem, your friends will be so pleased. I said: But you wrote that. Come on, said Captain Pjele, don't you recognize your own handwriting?

When he let me go, Captain Pjele complained about his kidneys and said: You're lucky you've got me.

At the next interrogation, Captain Pjele said: Today I'd like you to sing without a score. I sang, my absolute, certain fear remembered the tune. I never forgot it.

Captain Pjele asked: What does a woman do in bed with three men? I didn't reply. There must be goings on like at a dog's wedding, said Captain Pjele. But then you folk don't want to get married, that's something couples do, not packs. Which of them are you going to take as the father of your child?

I said: Talking doesn't get you pregnant. Come now, said Captain Pjele, it's an easy matter, getting a little Goldilocks.

Before I could go, Captain Pjele said: You're all bad seed. As for you, we're going to stick you in the water.

Bad seed, I thought—that was what Father saw when he took his hoe to the thistles. I wrote a couple of letters with commas after the greeting:

Dear Edgar,

Dear Georg,

The comma was supposed to be silent when Captain Pjele read the letters, to make him seal the letters again and send them on. But when Edgar and Georg opened them, it was supposed to cry out.

There was no such thing as a comma that could both keep silence and cry out. The comma after the greeting turned out much too thick.

I couldn't leave the parcel of books and letters behind the files in the office any longer. I took it to my seamstress to forget it there until I could find a safe place for it in the factory.

The seamstress was ironing. Her tape measure lay coiled on the table. The clock was ticking in the room. On the bed lay a floral-patterned dress. On the chair sat a young woman. The seamstress said: Tereza. I know her from the factory, I said, she'd had her arm in a cast for a long time. It wasn't until Tereza laughed that I looked at her. Now my right arm is all brown from the sun and the left one's completely white, said Tereza. If I wear long sleeves, no one will notice. The clock was ticking in the room. Tereza got undressed and slipped her brown arm into the floral-patterned dress. She swore, because she couldn't get it into the sleeve right away. The seamstress said: You won't turn a neck into a sleeve even if you swear.

When Tereza had the dress on she said: A year ago, every time I heard someone swearing, I would shut my eyes. My colleagues in the office saw me doing it. Each time someone swore, I shut my eyes. They said: That's so you can see our swearwords more clearly. But I shut them so as not to see them. When I got to work the next morning, there would be pieces of paper lying on my desk, covered with masterful phrases about cocks and cunts. When someone swore, I thought of the pieces of paper and had to laugh. They said I closed my eyes when I laughed, too. Then I started to swear myself. At first just in the factory.

The clock was ticking in the room. I'm not going to take this dress off, said Tereza, it keeps me warm. The seamstress said: It's your swearwords that do that. It's the heavy fabric, said Tereza. Floral fabric is always summery, said the seamstress, I would never wear it in winter. And now I swear everywhere, said Tereza. She took the dress off.

The clock was ticking in the mirror too. Tereza's neck was too long, her eyes too small, her shoulderblades too sharp, her fingers too fat, her bottom too flat, her legs too crooked. Everything about Tereza looked ugly reflected in the ticking of the clock. Ever since I hadn't been allowed to stroke the woolen tassels on my father's slippers, no clock had ticked so loudly.

Would you wear this dress in the winter? Tereza asked. The dress had no belt. I said yes, and saw that Tereza was ugly because the ticking of the clock was breaking her into small pieces. The next moment, without the mirror, the common and ugly things about Tereza became extraordinary. More beautiful than they would be in women who were obviously beautiful.

The seamstress asked me: How's your grandmother? I said: Singing.

Mother stands in front of the mirror, combing her hair. My singing grandmother goes and stands next to her. My singing grandmother touches Mother's black braid with one hand and her own gray braid with the other. She says: Now I've got two children, and neither one is mine. Both of you

99

deceived me. I thought you were blonde. She snatches the comb away from Mother, slams the door, and takes the comb out into the garden.

When Tereza took the cards off the dressing-table with the mirror, I knew why the clock in the room had been ticking so loudly. Everybody in the room was waiting. But not for the same thing. The seamstress and Tereza wanted me to leave so that they could begin turning the cards over. I wanted them to turn the cards over before I left. Not until the seamstress had told Tereza's fortune with the cards could I forget the box from the summerhouse without attracting attention.

The seamstress was better known for fortunetelling than for dressmaking. Most of her customers didn't tell her why they'd come. But the seamstress knew from looking at them that what they needed was luck for their escape, their flight.

There are some I feel sorry for, said the seamstress, they pay a lot of money, but I can't change fate. The seamstress poured a glass of water and took a sip. I can feel who believes in the cards, she said, putting the glass down. You believe in the cards, but you're afraid of my reading. The seamstress looked at my ear. I felt myself flush. You don't know your cards, she said, but you have to live with what's on them.

Whereas I see bad luck coming, and sometimes I don't have to swallow it.

The seamstress picked up her glass. There was a ring on the table, but not where the glass had been; it was in front of my hand. I felt myself shiver. I didn't speak. The seamstress drank a sip of water.

The river and the stones by the river. The lower fork, where the path ends. The place where you had to turn back if you wanted to take yourself back to the city in one piece. Usually everybody did turn back there, because they didn't want to feel the sharp stones through the soles of their shoes.

Every so often someone didn't turn back, because he wanted to go into the water. The reason, people said, wasn't the river, which was the same for everyone. The reason, they said, was in the individual who didn't want to turn back. He was the exception.

Because I didn't want to turn back this time, I walked out right into the middle of the sharp stones. That was a purpose. Not, as Kurt had written, a purpose come with empty pockets. My purpose was the opposite: I filled my pockets with two heavy stones.

The day before, I had gone to an apartment block I didn't know, to look down at the ground from a sixth-floor corridor window. There was no one around, it was high enough, I could have jumped. But the sky overhead felt too close. Just as later, by the river, the water was too close. I was like the old men's birds, driven crazy by the whistles. Death was whistling for me. Because I wasn't able to jump, I went back to the river the next day. And the day after.

Three pairs of stones lay on the bank all in a row—one for each day I had been to the river. Each time I had chosen a different pair. I didn't have to look for them long, many stones offered to sink with me. But they were all the wrong ones. They came back out of my pockets and onto the ground. And again I walked back into the city.

One of the books in the summerhouse was called: On Suicide. It stated that only one way of dying can fit into a given head. But I was caught in a cold circle between the window and the river. Death was whistling for me from afar, I needed to sprint to get to him. I almost had myself under control, only a tiny bit of me refused to go along. Maybe it was my heart-beast.

After Lola's death, Edgar had said: That was a resolute move. Compared to Lola I was ridiculous. I went back to the river one more time, to hide the pairs of stones among the other stones. Lola knew right away how to tie a sack with a belt. If she had wanted the sack with the river in it, Lola would have known how to choose a pair of stones. That sort of thing wasn't in any book. I was thinking as I read: Now I'll know how to go about it if I ever need death.

The sentences in the book were so tightly packed, it

was as though they would eventually do what was necessary. But when I pulled them over my skin, they tore and let me go. I laughed out loud as I parted the pairs of stones by the river. I had done something wrong with death.

I was so stupid, I drove away my crying with laughter. So stubborn that I thought: The river isn't my sack. We're going to stick you in the water wasn't going to work for Captain Pjele.

Edgar and Georg didn't come until the summer vacation. Neither they nor Kurt found out that death had whistled for me.

Kurt told me every week about the slaughterhouse. The workers drank warm blood when they slaughtered the animals. They stole organ meats and brains. At nightfall they tossed joints of beef or pork over the perimeter fence. Their brothers and brothers-in-law would be waiting there in cars to collect them. The workers hung cowtails on hooks to dry. Some would stiffen as they dried, others kept their suppleness.

Their wives and children are accomplices, Kurt said. The wives use the stiff cowtails for bottle brushes, and the children get the supple ones to play with.

Kurt wasn't shocked that I'd had to sing to Captain Pjele. He said: I've almost forgotten that nice poem. I feel like the refrigerator full of Lola's tongues and kidneys. But where I work, everyone is Lola's fridge, and the eating area is the whole village.

I tried to say bad seed and dog's wedding in the voice of

Captain Pjele. Kurt was much better at imitating it than I was. He started laughing so hard that he hacked up phlegm. Suddenly Kurt swallowed and asked: Where was the dog, why wasn't Pjele the dog there?

The sack with the river wasn't mine. It didn't belong to any of us.

The sack with the window wasn't mine either. Later, it would belong to Georg.

The sack with the rope would belong to Kurt, later still.

Edgar, Kurt, Georg, and I didn't know that at the time. You might say that no one knew it at the time. But Captain Pjele wasn't no one. Maybe, even then, Captain Pjele had two sacks in mind: First the sack for Georg, and later the sack for Kurt.

Maybe Captain Pjele wasn't yet thinking of the first sack, still less of the second. But again, maybe Captain Pjele had thought of them both and was carefully spreading them out over years.

We couldn't imagine the thoughts of Captain Pjele. The more we thought about them, the less we could fathom them.

Just as I had to learn to leave space between cold and nail-clippers in a letter, so Captain Pjele had to learn to spread out the deaths of Kurt and Georg over the years. Maybe.

I never knew what the right thing to say about Captain Pjele might be. And what might be said about me, I only knew by turns, sometimes after three tries. And even then it was still always wrong.

．． ．

Between winter and spring I heard about five corpses that got snagged on reeds in the river outside the city. Everybody talked about them, as if they were talking about the dictator's illnesses. They shook their heads and shuddered. Kurt, too.

Kurt had seen a man in some bushes by the slaughterhouse. The workers were having a break and had run into the main building to warm up. Kurt didn't go along, since he didn't want to watch them drinking blood. He walked up and down the courtyard, looking at the sky. When he turned around, he heard a voice. It was asking for clothes. When the voice stopped, Kurt saw a man in the bushes, his head shaved, and dressed only in long johns.

It wasn't until after the break, when the workers were standing up to their necks in the ditch, that Kurt went back to the bushes. He urinated, then dropped a jacket and a pair of trousers. There was no sign of the man with the shaved head.

That evening Kurt went by the bushes again; the clothes were gone. The police and the army were combing the area. The following morning they searched the village as well. The slaughterhouse workers said a convict's cap was found in the beet field behind the slaughterhouse.

The man probably wound up in the river that very night, said Kurt. I only hope he wasn't the one they fished up, he had my clothes on.

I had a bitter taste in my mouth. I had practiced picking

out stones for three river corpses. Perhaps one pair was for him. He isn't necessarily the one, I said.

In the factory I was translating instructions for hydraulic machinery. For me, the machines were one big dictionary. I sat at a desk. I seldom went into the machine rooms. The dictionary and the iron of the machines had nothing to do with each other. The technical diagrams looked to me like something cooked up by the tin sheep and both shifts of workers. The things the workers slapped together with their hands needed no names inside their heads. And so the workers grew old on the job, unless they happened to run away or keel over and die.

Between its covers, the dictionary included every machine in the factory. But I was excluded by all the cogs and screws.

The alarm clock stopped a little after midnight. The mother doesn't wake up till almost noon. She winds the alarm clock, it won't tick. The mother says: Without the alarm clock, there'll be no morning. She wraps the alarm clock in some newspaper and sends the child to Toni the clockmaker. Toni the clockmaker asks: When do you need it back? The child says: Without the alarm clock, there'll be no morning.

Then it's the following day. The mother wakes up

just before noon, and she sends the child out to collect the alarm clock. Toni the clockmaker tosses two handfuls of alarm clock into a bowl and says: This one has had it.

On her way home, the child reaches into the bowl and swallows the smallest cog, the shortest rod, the thinnest screw. Then the next-smallest cog. . . .

Ever since Tereza got the floral-patterned dress, she started coming to see me in the office daily. She didn't want to join the Party. My consciousness isn't sufficiently developed, she stated in the meeting, and besides I swear too much. They all laughed, said Tereza. I'm allowed to refuse, because my father was an official in the factory here. He cast every monument in the city. He's an old man now.

I saw a barren province in Tereza's face, in her cheekbones, or smack in the middle of her eyes, or around her mouth. A city child, who still used her hands as well as her words to speak.

Into that place where, in me, there was emptiness, Tereza would never venture within herself. Maybe just once, when she took a liking to me for no real reason. Maybe because I remained outside the gestures of my hands. Outside many of my words too. Not just the ones that Edgar, Kurt, Georg, and I had agreed on for our letters. Others were waiting in the dictionary, words that the workers and the tin sheep had agreed on. I wrote them to Edgar and to Georg: wing nut, gooseneck, dovetail.

Tereza spoke without guile. She talked a lot and thought little. Shoes, she said, and meant only shoes. If the door slammed in the wind, she swore as much as if someone had died while fleeing.

We ate together, and Tereza showed me the swearwords on the pieces of paper. She laughed till her little eyes were wet. She wanted me to laugh as well, and she looked at me. On the paper, I saw the innards of slaughtered animals. I was unable to go on eating. I had to tell her about Lola.

Tereza tore up the pieces of paper. I was in the great hall too, said Tereza, we all had to go.

We ate together every day, and every day Tereza wore a different dress. She only wore the floral-patterned dress one day. She had dresses from Greece and from France. Sweaters from England and jeans from America. She had powder, lipstick, and mascara from France, jewelry from Turkey. And whisper-thin nylons from Germany. The women who worked in the offices didn't like Tereza. You could tell what they were thinking when they saw Tereza. They were thinking: All those things that Tereza has are worth fleeing for. They became envious and bitter. They craned their necks and sang:

He who loves and leaves
shall feel the wrath of God

God shall punish him
with the pinching beetle
the howling wind
the dust of the earth.

They sang the melody for themselves and for their flight.
The curse was aimed at Tereza.

The people in the factory ate yellowish bacon and hard
bread.

On my desk, Tereza used her pudgy fingers to arrange
rows of translucent slices of ham, cheese, vegetables, and
bread. She said: I'm making you some little soldiers, so that
you'll eat something too. She lifted the little stacks from the
table between her finger and thumb and popped them in her
mouth.

I asked: Why do you call them little soldiers? She said:
That's what they're called.

Tereza's food suited her. It smacked of her father. He
ordered it in the Party cafeteria. It was delivered to his house
in a car every week, said Tereza. My father doesn't need
to go shopping, he makes the rounds of his monuments and
carries a shopping bag around town with him for no reason.

I asked: Does he have a dog?

The seamstress's children said: Our mother is seeing a customer. It was the first time I had met them. I wasn't curious
about them. They asked: Who are you? I said: A friend of

your mother's. I winced as I said it, because I realized I wasn't one.

The children had dark-blue lips and fingers. When the pencil is dry, the children said, it writes gray. But when you wet it with spit, it writes as blue as night.

I thought to myself: It's the first time the children are here, because it's the first time I've come without any ulterior motive, because I'm not here to forget anything.

But there was something I wanted to forget, the death of the madman by the fountain.

The man with the black bow tie lay dead on the asphalt where he had stood for years. People flocked round him. The withered bouquet was trampled underfoot.

Kurt had said, the city's lunatics never die. When they keel over, another one climbs out of the asphalt to take his place. The man with the black bow tie had keeled over. Two others had emerged from the asphalt, a policeman and a guard.

The policeman drove the onlookers away. His eyes glittered, his mouth was wet from shouting. He had brought along the guard, who was used to pushing people and hitting them.

The guard stood by the soles of the dead man's shoes and stuck his hands in his own coat pockets. The coat smelled new, of oil and salt, like the impregnated cloth in shops. Its sleeves were too short, as on all guards' uniforms. The guard's coat was present. The guard's new cap was present, too. Only the eyes under the cap's brim were absent.

Maybe, as he stood by the dead man, the guard was paralyzed by the memory of his childhood. Maybe he had a village in his head. Maybe he suddenly thought of his father, whom he hadn't seen for a long time. Or his grandfather, who was already dead. Or a letter full of his mother's illness. Or maybe he was thinking of his brother, who, ever since the guard left home, has had to herd sheep with red feet.

The guard's mouth was too big for the time of year. It hung open, as there were no green plums to stuff it with since in winter.

So close to the dead man, who after so many years was soon rejoining his wife under the earth, the guard couldn't give anyone a thrashing.

The seamstress's children wrote their names blue as night on a piece of paper for the umpteenth time. They squabbled over space in which to write. Their squabbling wasn't loud: You stink of onions. You've got flat feet. You and your crooked teeth. You've got pinworms up your ass.

Under the table, the children's feet didn't reach the floor. On the table the children's hands were jabbing at one another with pencils. The fury in their faces was entrenched and grown-up. I thought to myself: While their mother's running late, they're growing up. What will happen if, in a quarter of an hour, they grow up, push their chairs away from the table, and walk off? How can I tell the seamstress, when she gets back and puts down her key, that her children won't be needing that key anymore?

When I wasn't looking at the children, I couldn't tell

their voices apart. In the mirror I saw my face and the big, staring eyes of a nobody. They had no cause to look at me.

The seamstress came back and put the key down on the dressing table, the cards and the rolled-up tape measure on the other table. She said: My customer has a lover who comes all over the ceiling. Her husband doesn't know that the stains on the ceiling over the bed are sperm stains. They look like water marks. Yesterday he brought his cousin back with him from the night shift. Even though it was raining, they climbed up onto the roof to look for loose tiles. They found two, but not over the bed. The cousin said: If the wind blows on a slant, the rain falls on a slant as well. My customer's husband wants to repaint the ceiling tomorrow. I persuaded him to wait till spring, said the seamstress. You know, I told him, it'll only happen again the next time it rains.

The seamstress stroked the hair of one child. The other leaned its head against her arm, it wanted to be stroked as well. But the mother went to the kitchen for a glass of water. You little moles, she said, those pencils are poisonous, just dip them in water. When she took out a blank piece of paper, the child she'd stroked put out its hand. But she laid the paper on the table.

The boyfriend can carry half a bucket of water on his cock, the seamstress said, he showed me once. I warned my customer. Her boyfriend comes from the South, from Scornicesti. He's the youngest of eleven children. Six of them are still alive. A man like that means bad luck. I predicted Tereza's broken arm, too. You know, the two of you are very different, said the seamstress, but sometimes that can be a good thing. Everyone who knows me believes what I tell them.

A man was carrying a bucket out of a hunchbacked house onto the street. He left the gate open. There was pale sun in the courtyard. The water in the bucket was frozen. The man upended the bucket over a pothole and stomped on it. When he lifted the bucket up, there was a frozen rat in a cone of ice on the ground. Tereza said: When the ice melts, it'll run away.

The man disappeared back into the hunchbacked house without saying a word. The gate gave a creak and the pale sun was again shut in the courtyard. Once Tereza had stopped swearing, I asked: Is the river still that frozen as well?

There were many questions Tereza wouldn't answer. Some questions I would repeat more than once. Others I would never ask again, because I forgot them myself. There were also things I didn't forget and never asked about again because I didn't want Tereza to know that they mattered to me. I was saving them for a good opportunity. Then, when the opportunity came, I wasn't sure whether the opportunity really was a good one. I let time slip until Tereza had moved onto something else. Then any opportunity was gone, not just the good one. I had to wait for another good opportunity.

Some questions Tereza didn't answer because she talked too much. So much talking left her no time to stop and think.

Tereza was incapable of saying: I don't know. Whenever she should have said that, she would open her mouth and say something completely different. As a result, when Captain Pjele called the office that spring and summoned me to an interrogation, I still didn't know if Tereza's father made the rounds of his monuments with a dog or not.

I was afraid that Captain Pjele might come to the factory. Right after his call, I took the books from the summerhouse into Tereza's office. She was talking and laughing with colleagues and just put the parcel away in her closet. She didn't ask what was in the parcel.

Tereza took the parcel on trust, and I didn't trust her.

In the street with the hunchbacked houses, the first flies were sitting on the walls. The new grass was so green it hurt your eyes. You could see it growing. Each day as Tereza and I left the factory, it was a little bit taller. I thought: The grass along the street grows faster than the second cyclamen blossom in Captain Pjele's office during Georg's interrogation. And in between the houses stood trees so bare that the shadows of their branches made you hesitate over every step. Their shadows lay on the ground like antlers.

Work was over for the day. Our eyes weren't yet used to the harsh sun. There wasn't a scrap of leaf on any of the branches. The whole of the sky hung over our heads. Tereza grew lightheaded and wild.

Under a tree Tereza moved her head up and down so long that its shadow touched the antlers on the ground. Under the shadows stood a beast.

Tereza moved her back against the spindly tree trunk. The antlers shook, left their beast, and found it once again.

When winter was over, Tereza said, a lot of people took advantage of the first sunshine of the year to go for walks in town. While they were out walking, they saw a strange beast slowly entering the city. It came on foot, though it could also fly. Tereza put her hands in her pockets and flapped the skirts of her open coat like wings. When the strange beast arrived in the big square in the middle of the city, it beat its wings, Tereza said. People began to scream and fled in fear into the houses of strangers. Only two people remained in the street. They didn't know each other. The antlers flew off the head of the strange beast and settled on the railing of a balcony. Up there in the bright sunshine the antlers shone like the lines in someone's hand. The two people saw their entire lives written in those lines. When the strange beast beat its wings again, the antlers left the balcony and settled back on the wild animal's head. Then the strange beast trudged down the bright, empty streets, out of the city. When it was far away, the people emerged from the strangers' houses and went about their lives once again. The fear remained in their faces. It twisted their features. Those people were never happy again.

But the other two went about their lives and avoided all misfortune.

Who were those two people? I asked. I didn't want an answer. I was afraid Tereza might say: You and me. Hurriedly I pointed to a faded dandelion by her shoe. But Tereza sensed, like me, that we belonged together only where there were no secrets. We didn't belong together in such short words as you and me. She rolled her little eyes and said:

No one will ever know again
Who those two people might have been.

Tereza stooped and blew the dandelion seeds off their stalk. I didn't know what she was thinking as the feathers swirled off the white orb into the air. She buttoned up her coat to get away from her strange beast. Without a word, she started walking. And I felt as though I had to stay and tell Tereza that I didn't trust her.

A little further on, Tereza turned back to me, waved and laughed.

In the next street, we looked for four-leaf clovers. The clover was still too soft for pressing, but the leaves already had the white rings. I don't want to press it, said Tereza, I just need its luck.

Tereza needed a stem of lucky clover, and I needed its real name: trefoil. We searched the clover patch on our hands and knees. I happened to find the one stem that had four leaves instead of three. Because I don't need any luck, I said to Tereza. I thought of hands that had six fingers.

When the mother ties the child to the chair with the belts from her dresses, the devil's child is standing outside the window. It has two thumbs on each hand, side by side. The outer thumbs are shorter than the inner ones.

At school the devil's child is unable to write nicely. The teacher cuts off its outer thumbs and puts them in a preserving jar full of alcohol. In one classroom there are no children, only silkworms. The teacher puts the preserving jar in with the silkworms. Every day the children have to pick leaves from the trees in the village to feed the silkworms. They eat only mulberry leaves.

The silkworms eat mulberry leaves and grow, and the children see the thumbs in alcohol and stop growing. All the children in this village are smaller than the children in the next village. So the teacher says: The thumbs belong in the graveyard. After school, the devil's child goes with the teacher to the graveyard to bury its thumbs.

The hands of the devil's child turn brown from picking leaves in the sun. But at the base of its thumbs are two little white scars like fishbones.

Tereza stood in the sun with empty hands. I gave her the lucky clover. She said: It won't help me, because you're the one who found it. It's your luck. But I don't believe in it, I said, so you're the only one it can help. She took the clover.

I walked a step behind Tereza and repeated the word trefoil as we clattered along, over and over, until it became as tired as I was. Until it lost its meaning.

Tereza and I were already on the main road, which was

paved. Here and there a frail stalk grew out of a crack. The trams creaked slowly, the trucks drove fast, their wheels whirling like clouds of dust.

A guard took off his cap, he puffed up his cheeks, let the air out of his mouth, as though his lips were about to burst. His cap had made a sweaty red welt across his forehead. He looked at our legs and clicked his tongue.

To tease him, Tereza started walking just the way he was standing, as though she weren't walking on the pavement, but on top of the world. I was a little cold and could only walk the way people did in our country. I felt the difference between this country and the world. It was bigger than the difference between Tereza and me. I was the country, but she was not the world. She was only what people in this country thought of as the world when they wanted to flee.

At the time I still believed that in a world without guards people would walk differently from the way we do in our country. Where people are allowed to think and write differently, I thought, they will also walk differently.

My hairdresser is over there on the corner, said Tereza. Soon it'll be warm, and then we can go and get our hair dyed.

I asked: What color?

She said: Red.

I asked: Today?

She said: Now.

I said: No, not today.

My face was on fire. I wanted to have red hair. For my

letters though, I thought, I could borrow hair from the seamstress. Hers was blonde like mine, but longer. One of her hairs would do for two letters, I could cut it in half. But to take hair from the seamstress unnoticed would be harder than forgetting things at her place.

Sometimes there were hairs lying in the seamstress's bathtub. Ever since I'd begun putting hairs in my letters, I'd started noticing that kind of thing. There were more pubic hairs than scalp hairs in the seamstress's bath.

I was renting a room from an old woman. Her name was Margit, and she was a Hungarian from Pest. The war had driven her and her sister to this city. Her sister was dead and buried in the graveyard where I had seen the faces of the living in the photographs on the tombstones.

When the war ended, Frau Margit hadn't had the money to return to Pest. And later on they closed the border. I would only have drawn attention to myself if I'd tried to go back to Pest then, said Frau Margit. Back then Father Lukas told me that Jesus, too, was not at home. Frau Margit attempted a smile, but her eyes didn't obey her when she said: I'm fine right here, there's no one waiting for me in Pest anymore.

Frau Margit spoke German with a broad accent. Sometimes I expected her to break into song with the next word. But her eyes were too cold for that.

Frau Margit never explained why she and her sister had come to this city. She only explained how the *Mojics*, the

Russian soldiers, had come to the city, and how they went from house to house taking people's wristwatches. The *Mojics* put their arms to their ears, listened to the ticking, and laughed. They couldn't tell time. They didn't know that when a watch stopped ticking, you had to wind it. When their watches stopped, the Russians would say *Gospodin,* and throw them away. The *Mojics* were keen on watches, they would wear a dozen on each arm, said Frau Margit.

And every couple of days, one of them would stick his head in the toilet bowl, she said, and get a comrade to flush it. That was how they washed their hair. The German soldiers, on the other hand, were tiptop. Frau Margit's face got so soft when she thought of them that a hint of her girlish beauty returned to her cheeks.

Frau Margit went to church every day. Before meals she went over to the wall, lifted her face, and pursed her lips. She whispered something in Hungarian and kissed the iron Jesus on His Cross. Her mouth couldn't reach up to Jesus' face. She gave him a Hungarian kiss on that part of his belly that was covered by a loincloth. The loincloth was knotted at that part and the knot stood out far enough from the Cross so that Frau Margit didn't touch the wall with her nose when she gave Jesus his kiss.

Only when Frau Margit was in a temper and threw the potatoes that she later peeled for dinner out of their crate and against the wall, did she forget her Jesus and swear in Hungarian. But later, when the potatoes were cooked and on the table, she kissed the swearwords away on the place where Jesus wore his loincloth.

On Mondays the acolyte gave three short knocks on her

door. She opened it a crack, and he passed her a little bag of flour, a white cloth with a silver-and-gold chalice embroidered on it, and a big tray. When the acolyte's hands were free, he bowed and Frau Margit shut the door.

From the flour and water, Frau Margit kneaded dough for Communion wafers and rolled it as sheer as nylons over the whole table. Then she cut out the wafers with a tin ring. She spread out the scraps of dough on a newspaper. When the wafers on the table and the scraps of dough on the newspaper were dry, Frau Margit laid the wafers out in layers on the tray. Then she covered them with the white cloth, so that the chalice was in the middle. The tray sat on the table like a child's coffin. The dry scraps of dough Frau Margit swept into an old biscuit tin with the side of her hand.

Frau Margit carried the tray with the white cloth to Father Lukas in the church. Before she went out on the street with the Communion wafers, she had to find her black kerchief. I wonder what the devil I could have done with that rag this time, said Frau Margit.

Father Lukas gave her money for the wafers each week, and from time to time a black sweater he no longer wore. And from time to time a dress or scarf that his cook no longer wore. That's what Frau Margit lived off, that and the rent I paid for my room.

Frau Margit put the biscuit tin by her left hand while she read the newspaper she got from Frau Grauberg, or her prayer book. She would reach into the tin without looking, and eat.

If Frau Margit spent too long reading and ate too many wafer scraps, her stomach would get so holy that she would belch as she peeled the potatoes, and then she would swear even more. Since I've known Frau Margit, holy for me means a dry, whitish crackling in the mouth that makes you belch and swear.

Frau Margit had picked up her Jesus during an August pilgrimage, in the rush between the bus and the steps of the church where the pilgrims were headed, picking Him at random from a whole sack of Jesuses that were on sale. The Jesus she kissed was made of scrap off one of the tin sheep from the factory, the product of an off-shift cottage industry. The only righteous thing about the Jesus on her wall was that he was stolen property, a traitor to the State.

Like every other Jesus in that sack, this one had been converted into drink at a bodega table the day after the pilgrimage.

The window of Frau Margit's room overlooked the courtyard. The courtyard contained three large linden trees and—in their shadow, the size of a room—a neglected garden with a broken boxwood hedge and tall grass. On the ground floor of the house lived Frau Grauberg and her grandson and Herr Feyerabend, an old man with a black moustache. He often sat on a chair outside the door of his apartment, reading the Bible. Frau Grauberg's grandson played in the boxwood hedge, and every couple of hours Frau Grauberg would shout the same sentence into the courtyard: Come and eat. Her grandson would always shout back the same sentence: What are we having, anyway? At that Frau Grauberg would raise her hand at him menacingly and shout: Just you wait, I'll show you what you're going to get. Frau Grauberg and her grandson had moved here from the Mondgasse. She could no longer stay in the factory housing, because the mother of her grandson had died in the Mondgasse, following a Cesarean. There was no father. Looking at Frau Grauberg, you wouldn't know she'd lived in factory housing, said Frau Margit, Frau Grauberg is always so intelligently dressed when she goes out in the street.

Frau Margit also used to say: Jews are either very stupid or very smart. Being stupid or smart is nothing to do with knowing or not knowing things, she said. Some people know a lot, but you could never call them smart; others don't know much, but you could never call them stupid. Wisdom and stupidity come from God alone. Herr Feyerabend is very smart, I'm sure, but he stinks of sweat. That doesn't have anything to do with God.

The window of my room overlooked the street. I had to go through Frau Margit's room to reach my own. I was not supposed to receive visitors.

Because Kurt came to visit every week, Frau Margit would sulk for four days. She wouldn't say hello or anything else to me. By the time she resumed saying hello and other things as well, there would be only two days left until Kurt's next visit.

The first sentence Frau Margit always said to me when she came out of her sulk was: I don't want any *kurva* in my house. Frau Margit and Captain Pjele were of one mind: If a man and a woman have something to give each other, they jump into bed together. If you don't go to bed with that Kurt of yours, then it's just a waste of time. If you stop seeing each other, you won't have to worry about giving each other anything, and you won't need to take anything from each other, either. Go find someone else, said Frau Margit, men with red hair are all good-for-nothings. That Kurt looks like a real Don Juan, he's not a gentleman.

Kurt didn't think much of Tereza; you shouldn't trust her, he said, and he slammed his bandaged hand down on the table. He had a split thumb, an iron bar had landed on it. A worker dropped it on my hand, said Kurt. On purpose. It was bleeding. I licked the blood off with my tongue, so it wouldn't run down my sleeve.

Kurt had already drunk half his tea. I'd scorched my tongue and was still waiting for mine to cool. You're much too sensitive, Kurt said. They left me there wounded, they stood by the ditch and watched me bleed. They had eyes like thieves. I was afraid they'd lost their minds. The minute those people see blood, they gather round to drink, to drink me dry. And afterward they all denied it. They were mute as the ground they were standing on. That's why I quickly licked the blood off and swallowed and swallowed. I didn't dare spit it out. Then it got to me, I began to scream. I practically tore my mouth with screaming. They all belonged in the dock, I screamed, they had stopped being human a long time ago. They made me sick with all their blood guzzling. I told them that their whole village was one big cow's ass, which they slip into at night and slip out of again in the morning to guzzle more blood. That they lure their kids into the slaughterhouse with dried cowtails and intoxicate them with kisses that taste of blood. That the sky ought to fall in on their skulls and crush them. Then they turned their thirsty faces away from me. They were one big speechless herd in their loathsome guilt. I walked through the slaughterhouse halls looking for some muslin to tie up my thumb. The first-aid box didn't have anything but an old pair of glasses, some cigarettes, matches, and a tie. I found a handkerchief in my jacket, wrapped it round my thumb, and bound it on with the tie.

Then the herd slowly shambled into the building, said Kurt, one after the other, as though they didn't have feet, just big eyes. The slaughtermen, who were drinking blood, called them over. The herd shook their heads. That one day they shook their heads, said Kurt, the next day they'd forgotten my screaming. Habit turned them back into what they already were.

When Kurt fell silent, there was a crackling behind the door. Kurt looked at his bandaged hand and listened. I said, it's Frau Margit eating the scraps left from the Communion wafers. You shouldn't trust her, said Kurt, she snoops around when you're not here. I nodded. The letters from Edgar and Georg are in the factory, I said, with the books. I didn't say that the books were with Tereza. Kurt's bandaged hand looked like a misshapen lump of wafer-dough.

Mother rolls the strudel dough across the table. Her fingers are nimble. They snatch and pluck as if they were counting money. The dough turns into a thin tablecloth. Something shimmers through the dough on the table: A picture of Fa-

ther and Grandfather, both of them young. A picture of
Mother and my praying grandmother, my mother much
younger.

My singing grandmother says: The barber is outside, but
didn't we used to have a little girl living here with us once?
Mother points at me and says: Here she is, she's just grown
a bit.

I sat there exhausted, my eyes burning. Kurt propped his
head on his unbandaged hand. His hand pressed so hard it
made his mouth go crooked. It seemed to me that Kurt was
putting all his weight on the corner of his mouth.

I looked up at the picture on the wall: A woman forever
looking out the window. She was wearing a knee-length
hoopskirt and carried a parasol. Her face and legs had the
greenish color of someone who's just died.

When Kurt first came to visit me in this room and saw
the picture, I said: The skin of the woman in the picture
reminds me of Lola's earlobes, that's how green they were
when she was taken out of the closet.

During the summer I could see beyond the picture of the
newly dead woman. The thick leaves outside the window
tinted the light inside my room so that the color of recent
death disappeared. When the trees lost their leaves, I
couldn't stand the newly dead woman. I didn't allow my
hands to take the picture down because I owed the color to
Lola.

Then I'll take the picture down, said Kurt, but I pushed

him back into his chair. No, I said, it isn't Lola. I'm just glad it's not Jesus. I bit my lips, Kurt looked at the picture. We listened. Behind the door, Frau Margit was talking to herself aloud. Kurt asked: What is she saying? I shrugged my shoulders. She's either praying or swearing, I said.

I drank blood like the others in the slaughterhouse, said Kurt. He looked out on the street. Now I'm an accomplice too.

A dog was walking down the opposite side of the street. The man in the hat will show up any minute now, said Kurt, he follows me around whenever I'm in the city. The man showed up. He wasn't the same man who followed me. I might know the dog, I said, but I can't tell from here.

I wanted Kurt to show me his wound. You and your Swabian chamomile tea and sympathy, he said. You and your tight Swabian ass, I said.

We were surprised we could still muster such nasty expressions. But the hate was missing, the words couldn't hurt us. There was only a wry pity in our mouths. And instead of fury, an embarrassed pleasure that our minds had managed to come up with something after such a long time. We asked ourselves without using words whether Edgar and Georg, when they came back to the city, would still have enough life in them to be able to hurt us.

Kurt and I laughed out loud into the room, as if we had to take hold of each other before our faces started to twitch out of control. Before we each began to worry about mastering the corners of our mouths. While we laughed we watched each other's mouth. We knew that at any moment we would be abandoned, deserted by the other, by the controlled lips as much as by the uncontrolled twitches.

That moment came: I locked myself up in the pounding of my heart and was out of Kurt's reach. My coldness could not come up with any angry words, it couldn't come up with anything anymore. In my fingers, this coldness felt capable of violence. A hat passed by outside the window.

I think you'd like to be an accomplice, I said, but you're really just a show-off. You lick your thumb, while the rest of them drink pig's blood.

So what? said Kurt.

There was an exclamation mark after the greeting. I looked for the hair, first in the stationery, then in the envelope. There wasn't one. In my second wave of panic, I realized the letter was from Mother.

Behind my mother's back-pain I read: Grandmother has stopped sleeping nights. Only by day. She gets them mixed up. Grandfather can't get any rest. She never lets him shut his eyes, and he can't sleep in the daytime. At night she switches on the light and opens the window. He switches off the light, shuts the window, and lies back down. So it goes until it starts getting light outside. The window is broken. She says it was the wind—I ask you. No sooner is she out of the room than she goes back in again. She leaves the door open. If Grandfather doesn't move and just lets her carry on, she goes up to his bed. She takes his hands and says: You shouldn't sleep, your heart-beast isn't home yet.

Grandfather is worn out, it's risky for him at his age. And I'm dreaming like crazy. I'm plucking a red cockscomb in the garden. It's the size of a broom. The stalk refuses to break off, I pull and yank at it. The seeds spill out the end like black salt. I look at the ground, ants are crawling everywhere. They say if you dream of ants it means a rosary.

In the summer my singing grandmother ran away from home. She went through the streets calling out to each and every house. Her voice was loud. No one understood what she was shouting. When someone came out into the yard because of her shouting, she ran away. Mother went looking for her in the village, in vain. Grandfather was sick, so she couldn't stay out long.

After dark, when my singing grandmother came home, Mother asked: Where have you been? My singing grandmother said: At home. You've been in the village, said my mother, your home is here. She pushed my singing grandmother down into a chair: Who are you looking for in the village? My singing grandmother said: My mother. I'm your mother, said my mother. My singing grandmother said: You've never combed my hair.

My singing grandmother forgot her entire life. She had slipped back into her childhood. Her cheeks were eighty-eight years old. But her memory now ran along only a single track, and there she stood, a three-year-old girl chewing the corner of her mother's apron. When she came back from the village, she was as dirty as a child. Since she'd stopped singing, she'd taken to putting everything in her mouth. Her singing turned to walking. She was so restless, no one could control her.

When Grandfather died, she wasn't at home. During the funeral, the barber stayed in her room to look after her. She would only have disrupted the funeral, said Mother.

If I couldn't be there, I at least wanted to play chess while the coffin was being lowered into the ground, said the barber. But she wanted to run away. Talking to her didn't help, so I combed her hair. I ran the comb through her hair, and she sat and listened to the bells tolling.

When Grandfather was lowered into the ground, the crown imperial lilies were already flowering on Father's grave.

In the description of some hydraulic equipment, I came across the word transfinite. It wasn't in the dictionary. I could think of what transfinite might mean in human terms, but not in terms of machinery. I asked the engineers, and I asked the workers. They held small and large tin sheep in their hands and frowned.

Along came Tereza, I could see her red hair in the distance.

I asked: Transfinite?

She said: Finite.

I said: Transfinite.

She asked: How should I know?

Tereza was wearing four rings. The stones in two of them were red, as if they had fallen out of her hair. She put a newspaper down on the table and said: Transfinite, maybe it'll come to me during lunch; I'm having turkey today.

I unpacked my bread and my yellowish bacon. Tereza diced it and made two little soldiers. We ate, she pulled a face. It tastes rancid, said Tereza, I'll give it to the dog.

I asked: Which one?

She unpacked some tomatoes and a piece of turkey. Have some, she said, and made two little soldiers. She was already swallowing, I was still chewing. She pulled all the flesh from the bones.

Tereza pushed a little soldier into my mouth and said: We'll ask the seamstress about transfinite.

My distrust caused everything close to me to slide away. I struggled to grasp the truth and watched my fingers clutching at it, but in fact I didn't understand my own hand any better than Tereza's or Mother's. I understood it as little as I understood the dictator and his illnesses, or the guards and the passersby, or Captain Pjele and the dog Pjele. Nor did I understand any more about tin sheep and workers or the seamstress reading her cards. Not to mention flight and good and bad luck.

In the factory, a slogan was hanging from the gable that commanded the highest view of the sky and the deepest view of the yard:

Workers of the world, unite.

And down on the ground walked shoes that could only leave the nation by fleeing. Slippery shoes, dusty shoes, clattering or quiet, they marched up and down the pavement. I sensed that they knew of other ways and that one day they, like many other shoes, would cease walking underneath this slogan.

Paul's shoes had ceased walking here. The day before yesterday he hadn't shown up for work. He disappeared and his secret turned into gossip. Everyone thought they knew how he'd died. In his failed flight they saw a common wish that dragged one person after another toward death. They didn't give up the wish. When they said, He'll never come back, they meant themselves as much as they meant Paul. It sounded like Frau Margit saying: There's no one waiting for me in Pest anymore. But right after she'd fled, there might have been someone waiting in Pest after all.

Here in the factory, no one waited for Paul, not even for an hour. Bad luck, they said after he failed to return to work, like many before him. They stood in line, like people in a store. When death was served to someone, everyone moved up a place. What did the milk of the fog know about it, or the currents of air, or the curve of the tracks? A death as cheap as the hole in your pocket. You stick your hand in it, and your whole body has to go along. The more people died, the greater the obsession of those who remained.

The deaths of people fleeing were whispered about in a different way from the illnesses of the dictator. He would appear on television the same day and stave off the nearness of death with more record-length ramblings. Even as he spoke, a new illness was found, this one sure to finish him off.

The only thing they didn't know in the factory was the place of death: What was the last thing Paul saw of this world—corn? sky? water? or a freight train?

Georg wrote: The children can't say a single sentence without "Have to." I have to, you have to, we have to. Even when there's something they're proud of, they say: My mother had to buy me new shoes. And that's right. It's the same for me. I have to ask myself every night whether tomorrow will ever come.

Georg's hair slipped through my fingers. On the carpet I found only my own hairs and Frau Margit's. I counted the gray hairs, as though they would tell me how often Frau Margit came into my room. There wasn't a single hair of Kurt's in the room, even though he came every week. There was no depending on hairs, but I counted them just the same. And a hat was just going by outside the window. I ran over and stuck my head out.

It was Herr Feyerabend. He was shuffling his feet and pulled a white handkerchief out of his pocket. I withdrew my head, as if the white handkerchief could feel that someone like myself was staring at a Jew.

All Herr Feyerabend has is his Elsa, said Frau Margit.

I had told him once, as he was sitting in the sun without his Bible, that my father had been an SS-man who came back from the war, and that he hacked down his damn stupid plants, which were milk thistles. That right up until his death my father had sung songs to the Führer.

The lindens were blooming in the courtyard. Herr Feyerabend looked at the tips of his shoes, stood up, and looked at the trees. It makes me melancholy when they bloom, he said. All thistles have milk in them. I've eaten a great many, more than I've had cups of lindenflower tea.

Frau Grauberg opened the door. Her grandson went out to the street in white kneesocks, turned back at the gate—first facing her, then the two of us—and said: Ciao. And I said: Ciao.

Once Frau Grauberg, Herr Feyerabend, and I had watched the white kneesocks—more than the child—disappear, Frau Grauberg's door fell shut. Herr Feyerabend said: You heard it yourself, the children are saluting, just like they did under Hitler. Herr Feyerabend also paid close attention to words. Ciao for him was the first syllable of Ceauşescu.

Frau Grauberg is Jewish, he said, but she claims she's German. And you're afraid, so you return the greeting.

He didn't sit down again. He reached for the door handle, and the door flew open. A cat put her white head out of the cool room. He took her on his arm. Inside, I saw a table with his hat lying on it, the clock was ticking. The cat wanted to jump down. He said: All right, Elsa, let's go inside. Before he shut the door he said: Ah yes, thistles.

I explained to Tereza what an interrogation is. For no reason, as though I were talking to myself, I began to speak. Tereza clutched her gold chain with two fingers. She didn't move, so as not to blur the inky precision.

1 jacket, 1 blouse, 1 pr. trousers, 1 pr. nylons, 1 pr.

panties, 1 pr. shoes, 1 pr. earrings, 1 wristwatch. I was stripped naked, I said.

1 address book, 1 pressed lindenflower, 1 pressed clover-leaf, 1 ballpoint pen, 1 handkerchief, 1 mascara, 1 lipstick, 1 powder, 1 comb, 4 keys, 2 stamps, 5 tram tickets.

1 handbag.

Everything was entered under different headings on a single sheet. Everything except me, whom Captain Pjele failed to write down. He will lock me up. There won't be any list saying that I had in my possession when I arrived here 1 forehead, 1 pr. eyes, 1 pr. ears, 1 nose, 1 pr. lips, 1 neck. I know from Edgar, Kurt, and Georg that there are prison cells in the basement of the building. I wanted to take a mental inventory of my body to counter Captain Pjele's list. I only got as far as my neck. Captain Pjele will realize that some of my hair is missing. He will ask where the missing hairs are.

I was alarmed, because Tereza now had no choice but to ask me what I meant by the hairs. But I was unable to leave anything out. If you keep quiet for as long a time as I did with Tereza, you end up having to reveal everything. Tereza didn't ask about the hairs.

I stood in the corner completely naked, I said. I had to sing the song. I sang like water, nothing hurt me anymore, suddenly my skin was an inch thick.

What song? Tereza asked me. I told her about the books in the summerhouse and about Edgar, Kurt, and Georg. How we'd met after Lola's death. Why we had to tell Captain Pjele that the poem was a folk song.

Get dressed, said Captain Pjele.

It was as though I was putting on what had been written

down, so that the piece of paper would be naked when I was once again dressed. I took my watch off the table, and then my earrings. I buckled the watchstrap without fumbling and threaded in the earrings without a mirror. Captain Pjele walked back and forth in front of the window. I wanted to be naked for a while longer. I don't think he was looking at me. He was looking down at the street. The sky between the trees made it easier for him to imagine what I would look like when I was dead.

While I was dressing, Captain Pjele put my address book in his desk drawer. Now he has your address, too, I told Tereza.

I bent down and was tying my laces when Captain Pjele said: Cleanliness is next to godliness; one thing's for sure, you won't go to Heaven dirty.

Captain Pjele took the four-leaf clover off the table. He handled it carefully. Now do you believe you're lucky you've got me? he asked. I'm so lucky it makes me sick, I said. The fact that you're sick has nothing to do with your being lucky.

I didn't say a thing to Tereza about the dog Pjele, because I thought of her father. I didn't say that it was still a nice day when I went outside after my interrogation. And I didn't say that I couldn't understand how people could stroll and swagger about when they might be called up to Heaven at the drop of a hat. That trees propped their shadows against the houses. That people casually call this time of day early evening. That my singing grandmother was singing in my head,

Clouds—how many? Do you know?
Sail out where the four winds blow?

God Almighty counts each one,
None is missing when He's done.

That the clouds hung over the city like bright summer dresses. That the wheels of the tram threw up dust, and the streetcars let themselves be towed in the same direction I was going. That no sooner had the passengers got in than they sat down by the windows, just as if they were already at home.

Tereza let go of her gold chain. What does he want from all of you? she asked.

Fear, I said.

Tereza said: This gold chain is a baby. The seamstress went to Hungary for three days on a tourist visa, said Tereza, by bus with forty other people. The tour guide goes every week. He has his places, he doesn't need to trade on the street, he had the most luggage.

If you don't know your way around, it takes the first two days to sell and the third to buy. The seamstress had two suitcases full of cotton panties. They're light, said Tereza, you don't break your back lugging them around. They sell, too, but they're cheap, you don't make much on them. You need at least one suitcase full of crystal, crystal brings more money. The police are always patrolling the streets. Hairdressing salons are the best places to do business, the police don't bother you in there. The women under the dryers always have a bit of spare change and nothing to do while their hair's drying. You show them a handful of panties and a handful of glassware and they'll always buy something. The seamstress made a ton of money. On your last day, you buy. Gold's best. It's easy to hide and easy to sell at home for a good profit.

Women do better business than men, said Tereza, two thirds of the people on the bus were women. On the way home every one of them had a little plastic bag of gold stuffed up her snail. The customs men know, but what are they going to do about it?

I soaked the chain in a bowl of water overnight, said Tereza. I put plenty of detergent in, too. I wouldn't buy gold that had been in the snail of some woman I didn't know. Tereza swore and laughed. It seems to me the chain still smells, I'm going to wash it again. I'd ordered a gold clover-leaf to go with it, but the seamstress only brought two hearts for her children. In autumn, though, before it gets cold, she's going again.

Why don't you go yourself? I asked.

I'm not going to go lugging suitcases around and stuffing gold up my cunt, said Tereza. The journey home was at night. The seamstress got acquainted with one of the customs men. He told her which nights he was going to be on duty in the autumn. I'm sure the seamstress has something up her sleeve.

After the customs, there was nothing more to be afraid of, said Tereza. They all went off to sleep with gold between their legs. But the seamstress couldn't sleep, her snail hurt and she had to pee. The driver said: It's such a pain taking a load of women around, the moonlight makes them want to piss all the time.

• • •

The following day the seamstress's children were sitting at the table, and the hearts were dangling around their necks.

Necklaces are not suitable for children, said the seamstress. They're not allowed to wear them on the street. I bought them for later. When they're grown up, they won't forget me. The customer with the sperm stains on her ceiling went to Hungary, too, with her boyfriend. On the way there, she took up with the Hungarian customs official, for business reasons, said the seamstress. Her boyfriend paid her back for that later, he asked for a separate room in the hotel. But there wasn't one, and besides, he was down on the list with her. So he moved into my room. It wasn't my idea, but what was I supposed to do? said the seamstress. What was bound to happen, happened; I slept with him. I was really worried about the ceiling of the hotel room. The chambermaids check up on everything before you leave. My customer doesn't know about it. On the way home, he was sitting next to her again. He was stroking her hair and turning around to catch my eye. I don't want him to come knocking on my door one day—I don't want to lose my customer, I've known her for too long. When we got out of the bus for the customs control, he pinched my arm. To get rid of him, I made a play for the customs official. But also for business reasons, said the seamstress. When I go back in the autumn, I'll be able to take some electric mixers. They sell really well.

The seamstress asked me not to tell Tereza about the episode at the hotel. She pinched her cheek and said: Tereza wouldn't go on wearing the chain; as it is, she calls the chain my baby.

That's how it is, said the seamstress, when you spend all day doing business and you can't afford anything yourself. You feel miserable, and you want to know if you're still worth anything. Here at home, I wouldn't sleep with him. But over there, I earned it by working all day. So did he.

My customer came to me yesterday, said the seamstress, I had to read the cards for her. When she looks at me, my heart stops and the cards don't speak to me anymore. Nothing came out, and I wouldn't take any money. She pestered me. There are some things that you don't see right away, the seamstress said, they creep up on you like smoke. You'd better wait a day or two, I told my customer. But I'm the one who has to wait. The seamstress struck me as mature, relaxed, and calm.

Both children came running through the room, with their golden hearts. Their hair was flying. I saw two young dogs who would grow up and lose their way in the world, with mute golden bells tied to their collars.

The seamstress had one more gold chain for sale. I didn't buy it. I bought a cellophane bag striped with red, white, and green. It contained Hungarian sweets.

I gave the bag to Frau Margit, I thought it would make her happy. I thought of Kurt coming the next day. I wanted to appease her anger in advance.

Frau Margit read every word that was written on the bag and said: *Édes dràga istenem*—my sweet Lord. She had tears in her eyes, tears of joy, but the joy frightened her by showing her how she'd bungled her life, and by reminding her that it was far too late to return to Pest.

Frau Margit saw her life as a righteous penance. Her Jesus knew the reason, but He wasn't telling her. Frau Margit suffered, and for that reason she loved her Jesus more and more every day. The Hungarian bag stayed by her bedside. She never opened it. She read the familiar script on the bag over and over, as if it were a life that had passed her by. She never ate the sweets, because they would simply have vanished in her mouth.

Mother had been wearing black for two and a half years. She was still in mourning for my father, and now for Grandfather as well. She went into the city and bought herself a tiny hoe. For the graveyard, she said, and for the thick beds in the garden. It's too easy to damage the plants with a big hoe.

To me it seemed thoughtless to use the same hoe for vegetables and graves. Everything's thirsty, she said. This year's weeds have already gone to seed. The thistles are taking over.

Her black garb made her old. She sat next to me in the sun like a shadow. She propped her hoe against the bench. The trains run every day, and you never come home, she said. She unpacked bacon, bread, and a knife. I'm not hungry, she said, it's just to fill my stomach. She diced the bread and bacon. Grandmother is staying out in the fields even at night, she said, like a wild cat. We had one once, she hunted all summer and came back to the house in November with the first snowfall. Mother didn't chew much, she swallowed quickly. Everything that grows can be eaten, otherwise Grandmother would be dead already, she said. I gave up going out to look for her at night. There are so many paths, and I get scared in the fields. But it's no different being alone in the big house. You can't have a conversation with her, but if she came back at night, it would at least be another pair of feet in the house. Mother didn't put down her knife while eating, even though everything had already been cut into bite-size pieces. She needed it to speak with. The poppies didn't make it, she said, the corn stayed small, the plums are all shriveled up on the trees. When I've been in the city all day and get undressed at night, I'm covered with black-and-blue marks. I keep knocking into things. When I'm running around like that instead of working, everything seems to get in my way. In spite of the fact that there's so much more room in the city than in the village.

Then Mother got on the train. Its whistle was hoarse. When the wheels moved and the shadows of the train cars crept across the ground, the ticket collector leapt on board. He left one leg hanging in the air for quite some time.

Under the mulberry tree stood the discarded house chair, a withered grass pigtail dangling from its seat. Peeping over the fence were sunflowers, they had no crown and no black

142

seeds. They were stuffed and fluffy like pompoms. My father has bred them like that, said Tereza. Three pairs of deer antlers adorned the veranda.

I can't stand cauliflower soup, said Tereza, the whole kitchen reeks of it. Her grandmother took her plate, stomped over to the stove, and poured Tereza's soup back into the pot. The spoon rattled like a bellyful of angry cutlery.

I cleaned my plate. I think it was good soup. If I'd paid attention to the soup while I ate, I'm sure it would have tasted good. But I wasn't happy to be eating there.

Tereza's grandmother had set the plate down in front of me and said: Eat, then Tereza will eat too. You can't be as spoiled as she is. According to her, everything reeks—cauliflower, peas and beans, chicken livers, lamb and rabbit, it all reeks. I tell her: Your asshole reeks too. My son doesn't like to hear that. I'm not to say it in front of other people.

Tereza hadn't introduced me. Her grandmother didn't need my name; she saw a mouth in a face, so she gave me soup. Tereza's father stood with his back to the table, he ate his soup straight out of the pot, standing up. He probably knew who I was, so he didn't look round when I came in. He looked over his shoulder at Tereza and said: You swore again. The director didn't want to repeat your words, they were far too vulgar. You think your swearwords don't reek?

Whenever I see the factory, it's enough to make me swear, said Tereza. She reached into a bowl of raspberries, her fingers turned red. Her father slurped his soup. Every day you find a new way of hurting me, he said.

Her crooked legs, flat behind, and little eyes all came from him. He was big and bony, his head half-bald. When he visited his monuments, I thought, the pigeons could sit on his shoulders instead of the iron. As he slurped, his cheeks hollowed and his cheekbones climbed up under his little eyes.

Did he really resemble his monuments, or was it just that I knew he had cast them? One moment it was his neck and shoulders that looked to me like iron, the next it was his ears and his thumb. A bit of cauliflower fell out of his mouth. It stuck on his jacket, little and white as a tooth.

Even if the man had been short and fat, I thought to myself, with that chin he would have cast monuments anyway.

Tereza cocked her hip and took the bowl of raspberries under her arm. We went up to her room.

In the wall there was a narrow door covered with wallpaper. An autumn wood with birches and a stream. One birch tree had a door handle in its trunk. The water wasn't deep, you could see the bottom. The only stone that lay between the tree trunks was bigger than a pair of stones beside the river. No sky, no sun, but bright air and yellow leaves.

I'd never seen any wallpaper like it. It's from Germany, said Tereza. Her mouth was all bloody from the raspberries. So was the bowl on the table. Next to it was an open porcelain hand. It wore Tereza's rings on each of its fingers. Draped across the palm and the back of it were Tereza's necklaces, including the one from the seamstress.

Without the jewelry, the hand on the table would have looked like a stunted tree. But the jewelry glittered with a despair that could never have sprung from the wood or the foliage of trees.

I ran my fingertip up the birch trunk with the door handle, pushed the handle out of the way, and kept going. My aim was to reach the big stone in between the tree trunks as unobtrusively as I could. I asked: Where do you get to if you open the birch with the door handle? Tereza said: In the back of my grandmother's closet. Come on and eat some of these raspberries, otherwise I'll gobble them up all by myself, said Tereza.

How old is your grandmother? I asked. My grandmother comes from a village down in the south, said Tereza. She got pregnant while harvesting melons and didn't know by whom. She was a laughingstock in her village. So she got on the train. She had a toothache. The tracks only went as far as the station here. She got out, went straight to the nearest dentist, and stayed with him.

He was older than she was and lived alone, said Tereza. He had a decent income, while all she had was her secret. She didn't tell him she was expecting a baby. She thought he'd just assume it was premature. Then my father really was born premature. The dentist went to see her in the clinic. He brought flowers.

The day she was released, he didn't come. She took the baby home in a taxi. He wouldn't let her in. He gave her the address of an officer. She became a servant.

For years the officer used to go to her at night. My father pretended to be asleep. He understood that that was the only reason he was given everything the officer's children were given. He was allowed to call the officer Father when there was no one around. He was allowed to eat at the same table. One day, when the officer's wife was screaming at my grandmother because the glasses weren't clean, my father said: Father, give me some water. The officer's wife looked at the boy, then at her husband. He's your spitting image, she said.

She knocked the knife out of my grandmother's hand and started carving the rabbit herself.

Everybody ate while my grandmother packed. With the suitcase in her hand, she picked her child, whose cheeks were bulging with meat, up off the chair. The officer's children wanted to go to the door, but the officer's wife wouldn't allow them to leave the table. They waved with their white napkins. The officer didn't dare glance at the door.

The dentist married again twice, said Tereza. Both wives left him because they wanted children. He couldn't have any. He would have been happy with my grandmother, if only he'd allowed himself a little deception. When he died, my father inherited his house.

Do you want to have children? Tereza asked me back then. No, I said. Imagine, you eat raspberries, duck, and bread, you eat apples and plums, you swear and you carry machine parts back and forth, you ride on the tram and you comb your hair. And all that becomes a child.

I still remember looking at the door handle in the birch tree. And how, still invisible to the eye, the nut was already there, under Tereza's arm. It took its time, it swelled and grew.

The nut grew against us. Against all love. It was ready to

betray us, it was impervious to guilt. It devoured our friendship before it killed Tereza.

Tereza's boyfriend was four years older than she was. He was studying in the capital. He was in medical school.

Before the doctors knew that the nut had spread to Tereza's breast and lungs, but after they already knew that Tereza couldn't have children, the student became a full-fledged doctor. He wanted children, he told her. That was just the tip of the corner of the truth. He left Tereza in the lurch so that she wouldn't die on him. He had learned enough about death.

I was no longer in the country. I was in Germany and received Captain Pjele's death threats by mail or by long-distance telephone. The letterheads showed two crossed axes. Each letter contained a black hair. Whose?

I looked at the letters closely, as if the killers Captain Pjele would send were sitting between the lines, looking up into my eyes.

The telephone rang, and I picked it up. It was Tereza.

Send me some money, I want to visit you.

Are you allowed to travel?

I think so, yes.

That was our conversation.

Then Tereza came to visit. I met her at the station. Her face was hot, my eyes were moist. On that station platform, I wanted to touch Tereza everywhere at once. My hands were too small for me, I saw the ceiling above Tereza's hair and felt myself floating up toward it. Tereza's suitcase pulled on my arm, but I carried it as if it were full of air. Not until we were on the bus did I notice that my hand had been rubbed red by the suitcase handle. I grasped the handrail where Tereza had her hand. I felt Tereza's rings within my hand. Tereza didn't look out the window at the city, she looked me in the face. We laughed as if the wind was giggling through the open window.

In the kitchen Tereza said: Do you know who sent me? Pjele. There was no other way I could have come. She drank a glass of water.

Why did you come?

I wanted to see you.

What did you promise him?

Nothing.

Why are you here?

I wanted to see you. She drank another glass of water.

I said: I'd be perfectly right to throw you out.

Singing in front of Captain Pjele was nothing compared to this, I said. Undressing in front of him didn't make me as naked as you have.

But it can't be such a bad thing that I want to see you, said Tereza. I'll make up something to tell Pjele, something of no use whatsoever. We can make it up together, you and I.

148

You and I. Tereza had no sense that you and I were finished. That you and I couldn't be spoken in one breath. That I was unable to shut my mouth because my heart was pounding in it.

We drank coffee. She drank it like water, she never let the cup leave her hand. Maybe she's thirsty from the trip, I thought to myself. Maybe she's been thirsty ever since I went to Germany. I saw the white handle between her fingers and the white rim of the cup against her lips. She drank so quickly, it was as though she wanted to drink up and leave of her own accord. Send her packing, I thought to myself; but she sat there, feeling her face with her hand. How can you send someone packing just as that someone is beginning to stay?

For me it was like being in front of the seamstress's mirror again. I saw Tereza in pieces: two little eyes, a long neck, pudgy fingers. Time stood still; Tereza should go but she should leave her face here, because I missed it so. She showed me the scar under her arm where they'd cut out the nut. I wanted to take the scar in my hand and stroke it, without Tereza. I wanted to rip my love out of me, throw it on the floor and stamp on it. Quickly lie down where it was lying and let it crawl back through my eyes into my head. I wanted to pull the guilt off of Tereza as if it were a badly made dress.

Her thirst quenched, she drank a second cup of coffee more slowly than the first. She wanted to stay for a month. I asked about Kurt. He's got nothing but the slaughterhouse in his head, said Tereza, talks about nothing but drinking blood. I don't think he likes me.

Tereza wore my blouses, my dresses and skirts. She went into town with my clothes instead of with me. The first evening I gave her the key and some money. I said: I don't have any time. She was so thick-skinned, my excuse just bounced off her. She went off on her own and came back with bags full of shopping.

In the evening I found her next to the bathtub, about to wash my clothes. I said: It's all right, you don't have to give them back.

After Tereza had left the house, I went out too. Apart from the pounding in my throat, I could feel nothing. I stuck to the surrounding streets. I avoided shops, so I wouldn't run into Tereza. I didn't stay out long, I came back before she did.

Tereza's suitcase was locked. I found the key under the carpet. In the inner compartment of the suitcase I found a telephone number and a new key. I went to my own front door, the key fit. I dialed the number. A voice said: Romanian Embassy. I locked the suitcase and put the suitcase key back under the carpet. I put the front-door key and the telephone number in my desk drawer.

I heard the key in the door, Tereza's footfall in the corridor, the door to her room opening. I heard the rustle of shopping bags, the door to her room, the kitchen door, the refrigerator door. I heard the clink of knife and fork, the running tap, the fridge door slamming shut, the kitchen door, the door to her room. I swallowed hard at each noise. I felt hands taking hold of me, every noise gripped me.

Then my door opened. Tereza stood there with a half-eaten apple in her hand and said: You've been in my suitcase.

I took the key out of the desk drawer. Is this your something of no use whatsoever to Pjele? I said. You've been to get my key copied. Your train leaves tonight.

My tongue felt heavier than the rest of me. Tereza dropped her apple. She packed her suitcase.

We went to the bus stop. There was an old woman waiting there with a square handbag and her ticket in her hand.

She walked up and down saying: There ought to be one any minute. Then I saw a taxi and flagged it down, so that no bus would ever come, so that I wouldn't have to sit or stand there waiting with Tereza.

I climbed in next to the driver.

We stood on the platform, she wishing she could stay another three weeks and I wishing that she could vanish on the spot. There were no goodbyes. Then the train pulled out, and there was no hand waving, either inside or outside.

The tracks were empty, my legs felt weaker than two threads. I walked home from the station. It took me half the night. I wished I would never get there. I don't sleep at night anymore.

I wanted love to grow back, like the grass when it's mown

down. To grow differently, if need be, like children's teeth, like hair, like fingernails. To spring up at will, wild and untended. The chill of the sheets made me shudder, and so did the warmth that followed when I lay down.

When Tereza died, six months after her return home, I wanted to give my memory away; but to whom? Tereza's last letter arrived after her death:

Now all I can do is breathe like the vegetables in the garden. I have a physical longing for you.

My love for Tereza did grow back. I forced it to, and I had to protect myself. To protect myself from Tereza and me, the way we had been before her visit. I had to tie my hands. They wanted to write and tell Tereza that I still remembered the two of us. That the cold inside me stirs up love, against all reason.

After Tereza had left, I spoke with Edgar. He said: You shouldn't write to her. You've drawn a line. If you write and tell her how much you're suffering, it will start all over again. Then she'll come back to visit you. I think Tereza's known Pjele as long as she's known you. If not longer.

Why and when and how does tightly tied love get mixed up with murder? I felt like shrieking curses beyond my command.

He who loves and leaves
shall feel the wrath of God
God shall punish him
with the pinching beetle
the howling wind
the dust of the earth.

Shrieking curses, but in whose ear?

Today the grass listens when I speak of love. It seems to me that this word isn't honest even with itself.

But back then, when the birch with the door handle in it was too far away from the stone on the forest floor, Tereza opened the wardrobe and showed me the parcel from the summerhouse. It's better off here than in the factory, she said. If you have anything else, just bring it over. Same goes for Edgar, Kurt, and Georg, of course, she said. I have plenty of space here, said Tereza as we picked raspberries in her garden.

Her grandmother was sitting under the mulberry tree. There were a lot of snails on the raspberry bushes. Their shells were black-and-white-striped. Tereza grabbed too many raspberries too firmly, and a lot of them were squashed. In some countries they eat snails, said Tereza. They suck them out of their shells. Tereza's father walked out onto the street with his white canvas bag.

Once again Tereza mixed up Rome and Athens, Warsaw and Prague. For once, I didn't bite my tongue: You remember the different countries by your clothes. But you move the cities around any way you want. You should look at an atlas sometime. Tereza licked the squashed raspberries off her rings: And how has knowing any of this ever helped you? she said.

Her grandmother was sitting on the chair under the mulberry tree. She was listening to us and sucking on a sweet. When Tereza carried the full bowl past her, the sweet had stopped moving from cheek to cheek. She had fallen asleep, and her eyes were nearly shut. The sweet was lodged in her right cheek, it looked as if she had a toothache. As if she were dreaming of the tracks coming to an end, the way they had on the train back then. And in her dream under the mulberry leaves she was starting her life afresh.

Tereza had cut five sunflowers for me. Because of the mixed-up cities, they were as uneven as the fingers on a hand. I wanted to give them to Frau Margit because I came back late. But also because Edgar, Kurt, and Georg were coming in a week.

The Hungarian bag lay next to Frau Margit's bed. Jesus looked down into her illuminated face from the dark wall. Frau Margit refused the flowers. They're ugly, she said, they have no heart and no face.

On the table lay a letter. Behind my mother's back-pain was written:

On Monday morning I laid out some clean clothes for Grandmother. She put them on and went out into

154

the fields. I put the dirty ones to soak. One pocket was full of rosehips. In the other were two swallow's wings. My God, maybe she ate the swallows. It's a disgrace to let yourself go like that. Maybe you can talk to her. Maybe, now that she's stopped singing, she'll recognize you. She was always fond of you, she just didn't know who you were. Maybe she'll remember. She never could abide me, anyway. Come home, I don't think she has much longer.

Edgar, Kurt, Georg, and I sat in the boxwood garden in the courtyard. The lindens were tossing in the wind. Herr Feyerabend was sitting outside his door reading his Bible. Frau Margit had sworn as I went out into the yard with Edgar, Kurt, and Georg. I didn't care.

Georg gave me a round green board with a handle. On the board were seven yellow, red, and white chickens. They had strings running through their necks and bellies that were connected to a wooden ball hanging underneath the board. When you held the board in your hand, the ball swung back and forth. The strings tautened like the ribs of an umbrella. I tilted the board in my hand, and the chickens dipped their heads and raised them again. I heard their beaks clattering on the green board. On the underside of the board, Georg had written:

Directions: At first sign of unbearable sadness, tilt the board in my direction

Your butcher bird

The green is grass, said Georg, the yellow dots are corn-kernels. Edgar grabbed the board out of my hand, read the directions, and tilted the board. I saw the ball fly. The chickens went mad. Their beaks pecked furiously. We laughed so hard we could scarcely keep our eyes open.

I wanted to tilt the chickens while the others were obliged to watch. It was my board.

The child leaves the house where there are only grown-ups, to go play with the other children. She carries as many toys as she can, in her hands, in her pockets. Even in her underpants and up her dress. She empties out her dress and underpants, and spreads out her toys. Then, when the others start to play, the child can't stand to have her toys played with by anyone else.

The child is transformed by envy, because others are better at playing. By selfishness, because others are grabbing things that belong to her. But also by fear, that she will be left alone. The child doesn't want to be envious, selfish, or fearful, and becomes all the more so. She has to bite and scratch. An obstinate brute who drives the children away and spoils the games she had been looking forward to.

And then alone again. The child is ugly and more forlorn than anything in the whole world. She needs both hands to cover her eyes. The child wants to leave her toys, to give them all away. She waits for someone to grab them. Or to pull her hands away from her eyes, return bite for bite and scratch for scratch. Grandfather said: Tit for tat is no sin. But the children don't bite and scratch her. They shout: You can go shove your toys, we don't need them anyway.

There are days when the child hopes her mother will beat her. She walks fast, she's in a hurry to get home while the guilt is still fresh.

Her mother knows why the child has come home so quickly. She doesn't touch the child. Across the endless distance between her chair and the doorway she says: They've had it up to here with you, you can go and eat your toys for all they care. You're too stupid to play with.

And I was tugging at Edgar's arm again: You're breaking the strings, give me back the chicken-torture. They all yelled: Chicken-torture. Georg said: You Swabian chicken-torture. I screamed for the board, You're breaking the strings. I was too old for such childish selfishness, but the obstinate brute once again had me in its grip.

Herr Feyerabend got up from his chair and went in to his room.

Edgar held his hand up over my head. I saw the ball flying under the chickens. They're feeding on the fly, cried Edgar. They're feeding on flies, yelled Kurt. They're flying feasts, cried Georg. They were beside themselves, their brains were spinning in their heads like the ball on the string. How badly I wanted to step outside myself and be with them. Just don't spoil the game, don't steal their madness. Surely they must know, I thought, that we soon won't have anything left except who and where we are. And I caught Edgar's wrist in my teeth, tore the chicken-torture out of his hand, and scratched his arm.

Edgar licked off the trickle of blood, and Kurt stared at me.

Frau Grauberg called into the yard: Come and eat. Her grandson sat high up in the linden and called: What are we having anyway? Frau Grauberg waved her hand at him: Just you wait, I'll show you what you're going to get. At the foot of the linden lay a sickle. A rake was hanging from the lowest branch.

When the boy had climbed down from the tree and was standing in the grass next to the sickle, the rake was still swinging on the branch. Show me the chicken-torture, he said, and Georg said: It's not for children. The boy pouted and put his hand between his legs: I'm growing hair there. I said: That's normal. My grandmother says I'm growing into a man too quickly. And the boy ran off.

That boy ought to get lost, said Edgar, I don't want him hanging around with us. What will they say, I wondered, if Tereza decides to turn up? We had agreed that she might turn up, just by chance.

Kurt pulled a couple of bottles of schnapps out of his big traveling bag and a corkscrew from his inside pocket. Frau Margit won't let me have any glasses, I said. We drank out of the bottle.

Kurt showed us his photographs of the slaughterhouse. One was of meathooks, with cowtails dangling from them. These are the stiff ones used for washing bottles, and those are the supple ones that children play with, said Kurt. In another picture a calf was lying down. Three men were sit-

158

ting on it. One right at the front, on its neck. He was wearing a rubber apron and holding a knife in his hand. Behind him stood another man with a heavy hammer. Other men crouched in a semicircle. They held coffee cups in their hands. In the next picture, the sitting men were holding the calf by its ears and legs. In the next one, the knife was slitting its throat, the men were holding their coffee cups to catch the stream of blood. In the next picture they were drinking. Then the calf was lying on the slaughterhall floor alone. The cups stood in the background on the windowsill.

One picture showed freshly dug earth, picks and shovels, crowbars. A bush at the back. That's where the man with the shaved head was sitting in his underwear, said Kurt.

Kurt showed us pictures of his workers. At first, he said, I didn't understand why they all ran into the slaughterhall so fast. My office is on the other side of the building, the window looks out on the field: sky, trees, shrubs, and cattails, that's what I was supposed to be looking at during my break. They didn't want to let me into that one hall. All the others, yes, but not that one. Now they don't care if I watch them. Georg opened the second bottle. Edgar arranged the pictures in the grass. They were numbered on the back.

We hovered over the pictures like the men over the calf. I've got similar pictures of cows and pigs, said Kurt. He showed me the worker who had dropped the iron bar on his hand. He was the youngest. Kurt wrapped the pictures in newspaper. He took his toothbrush out of his jacket pocket. Pjele's been round to see me, he said. Will you forget the pictures at the seamstress's sometime? Even better would be Tereza's, I said, bring all your others, too.

Who is that? asked Georg. I opened my mouth to reply, but Kurt interrupted me: Another seamstress type.

Women always need other women to lean on, said Edgar. They become friends in order to hate each other better. The more they hate each other, the more inseparable they become. I see that in the women teachers. One of them whispers while the other lends an ear, and her mouth gapes open like a cracked prune. The bell rings, and they can't bear to part from each other. They stand together outside the classroom door, mouth and ear, while half the lesson time goes by. In the break they keep it up.

It can only be about men, said Georg. Edgar laughed: But most of them just have one, of course . . . and another on the side.

Edgar and Georg were the men on the side for a couple of women teachers. Outside, they said in the open air. They blushed a little and looked at Kurt and me.

And I was a woman on the side—just for the winter, because the man was no longer around once the winter was gone.

He never spoke of love. He thought of a stream, and told me I was a straw for him. But if I was a straw, I was a straw lying on the ground. That's where we lay every Wednesday after work, in the woods. Always on the same spot, where the grass was tall and the earth firm. The grass didn't stay tall. We made love hurriedly, feeling heat and frost on our skin at the same time. The grass stood up again afterward, I don't know how. And we counted, I don't know why, the crows' nests in the black acacia trees. The nests were empty. He said: You see? There were holes in the fog. They closed soon after. My feet felt the cold most, no matter how much we tramped through the woods. The frost began to bite even before it got dark. I said: But they'll come back to sleep, they're still out in the fields eating. Crows live to be a hundred.

The drops on the boughs no longer glittered. They had frozen into long noses. I didn't know how the light disappeared, although I watched it happen for a whole hour. He said there were things the eyes couldn't make sense of.

When it was very dark, we walked to the tram and rode back into town. What he said on Wednesdays when he got home so late, I don't know. His wife worked in the detergent factory. I never asked him about her. I knew she wouldn't be left alone because of me. With this man, it wasn't a question of taking him away. I only needed him on Wednesdays in the woods. Sometimes he told me about his child—that he had a stammer and lived in the country with the in-laws. He visited him every Saturday.

Each Wednesday the crows' nests were empty. He said: You see? He was right about the crows. But not about the straw. In the forest, a bit of straw on the ground was trash. That's what I was for him, and he for me. Of course, even a piece of trash can offer some footing when you never know where you are.

He was somebody from Tereza's office, who one day no longer turned up for work. Under the crows' nests, he suggested that he and I flee across the Danube together. He was banking on the fog. Others banked on wind, night, or sunshine. That's the way it is, the same thing means a different thing to each person. Like a favorite color, I said. But I thought: Like a way of dying.

Somewhere in our acacia wood there must also have been a tree with a door handle in its trunk. I saw that tree trunk later, not then in the woods. Maybe it was too close to me. But he knew that tree, and he opened that door.

By the following Wednesday he had died while attempting to flee with his wife. I kept waiting for some sign of life. It wasn't because of love that I missed him. But once you've shared a secret with a person, he can't just up and die. Even then I asked myself why I went into the woods with him. To lie under his body for a while in the thick grass, kick and writhe out of my locked-up flesh, and afterward not crave his eyes even for a second—perhaps it was that.

Months later, his name turned up on a scrap of paper in the medical records department. Tereza, who was always poking around everywhere in the factory, saw the official notice. It listed his name, occupation, home address, date of death. Cause of Death: natural death—heart failure. Place of Death: home. Time: 17:20. The coroner's stamp, a blue signature.

The same scrap of paper with his wife's name on it turned up at the detergent factory, where Tereza knew a nurse. It gave the same date of death: natural death—heart failure, 12:20, at home.

Tereza said: You ask about him so much, and you know him better than most. Everyone knew you had something going with him. It was the first thing I knew about you. When the two of us first met at the seamstress's, he had been in to see her. He was just leaving when I arrived. She read his cards. It doesn't matter anymore, said Tereza, but I wouldn't have trusted him.

Captain Pjele never asked me about him. Maybe after all there was something that Captain Pjele didn't know. But I went into the woods so many times, how could Captain Pjele not have known about it? Maybe Captain Pjele talked to him about me. But he never asked me things when we were in the woods, he didn't really know anything about me. That struck me, precisely because I didn't love him.

But maybe he knew enough to tell Captain Pjele that I could sing, if I had to.

You have your loves, they smell of wood and iron, said Kurt. I don't, but it's better that way. I can't sleep with the wives and daughters of the blood-guzzlers, he said, as we put together the list of people we had heard of who had been killed while attempting to flee. It covered two pages. Edgar sent the list abroad.

Most of the names I got from Tereza, a few from the seamstress. Her client with the sperm-stains and her husband and his cousin all were dead.

Georg was cutting the grass with the sickle. Our heads were heavy from the list of names and from the schnapps. Georg got a little wild, and we watched him. He spat on his hands, hopped behind the rake, and made some hay. Then the rake was back dangling from the branch. Georg pulled his toothbrush out of his trouser pocket. He spat on it and combed his eyebrows.

I asked who owned the summerhouse. Edgar said, A customs official. He had a lot of foreign currency. He kept it hidden in a chandelier at my parents' house so no one could find it. My father knows him from the war. Now he's retired, he'll smuggle the list through the customs. His son gave me the key, he lives in the city.

Papers had disappeared from Edgar's room. He had a spare copy of the list. Not at home, he said. But he didn't have his poems anymore. Not even in my head, said Edgar.

Tereza didn't come that afternoon. I gave her the photographs taken in the factory. Her father had been warned about me the day before. I was exerting a harmful influence on his daughter, Captain Pjele had told him, the only thing missing was a red light in my window.

I acted dumb, said Tereza, and asked my father if that was a reference to the Party. My father said: The Party isn't a brothel.

Edgar, Kurt, and Georg were long gone. The cut grass dried in the sun. Every day I watched the pile get lighter and smaller. It had turned into hay. The stubble had started springing up again.

One afternoon the sky turned black and fire-yellow. At the edge of the city, lightning crossed swords, and it thundered. Wind tugged at the lindens and tore off smaller branches. It dropped them on the boxwood and whisked them up into the air again. They jerked about, the boxwood cracked. The light was coal and glass. You could put your hand out and touch the air.

Herr Feyerabend was standing under the trees, stuffing hay into a blue cushion. The wind stole bunches of it out of his hand. He chased them and caught them underfoot. In this light he looked like a silhouette. I was afraid the lightning might see him and strike. When heavy drops of rain started to fall, he ran for shelter. For my Elsa, he said, and carried the cushion into his room.

B ehind Mother's back-pains I read: Frau Margit has written me a letter. She says you're going out with three different men. Thank God, they're all German, but it's still whoring, isn't it? You pay for your child to be educated in the city over many years, that's fine. And to thank you, she turns into a whore. I expect you have another one in the factory too. God forbid that you appear on my doorstep with some Romanian and say: This is my husband. The barber used to cut hair in the city, you know, and he said at the time that educated women are no better than spittle. But you always think your own daughter will turn out differently.

T he beeswax was boiling in the pot, the bubbles popping and frothing round the wooden spoon like beer. On the table, among the dishes and brushes and jars, was a photograph. The beautician said: That's my son. The boy was holding a white rabbit in his arms. The rabbit's gone, she said, it ate wet clover. His stomach burst. Tereza swore. We didn't realize, said the beautician, we picked it with the dew still on. The fresher the better, we thought. With the spoon, she smeared a broad strip of wax up Tereza's leg. It's high time, she said, it's sprouting like dill on your calves. As she peeled the wax off, Tereza closed her eyes. We would have slaughtered the rabbit later anyway, said the beautician, but it wasn't to be. The strip of wax tore. She pulled on the loose end. The first strip hurts, but then you get used to it, there are worse things, said the beautician.

Worse things, and I could have told her what. And that was partly why I wasn't sure I still wanted to get myself waxed.

Tereza folded her hands underneath her head and looked at me. Her eyes were dilated, like a cat's. You're afraid, she said. The beautician smeared a spot of wax into Tereza's arm-pit. By the time the deft fingers pulled it off again, it had sprouted a hairbrush.

Rabbits are pretty, especially white ones, said Tereza, but their meat reeks just as much as that of the gray ones. Rabbits are clean animals, said the beautician. Tereza's armpit was bare. In it I saw a lump the size of a nut.

The chicken-torture lay next to the dictionary. Tereza tilted it every day before we ate. When she came in the door, she said: I've come to feed the chickens. And each time she asked me whether I'd managed to find out the Romanian name for the bird in Georg's directions. But I could only give Tereza a literal translation: butcher bird. She couldn't find that name in any Romanian dictionary.

I had a German nanny once, said Tereza. She was old, because my grandmother wouldn't have a young nanny in the house who might tempt my father. The old woman was strict and had a quincy smell. She had long hair growing on her arms. I was supposed to learn German from her. *Das Licht,* the light; *der Jäger,* the hunter; *die Braut,* the bride. My favorite word was *Futter,* fodder, because it reminded me of the Romanian word for fuck. It didn't have that quincy smell:

She gives us milk and butter,
We give her fresh green fodder.

The nanny also used to sing:

Home now, children, for the night
Mama's blowing out the light.

She translated the song for me, but I kept forgetting it. It was a sad song, and I wanted to be happy. When my mother sent her to market, she would take me with her. On the way home I was allowed to look with her at the pictures of the brides in the photographer's shop window. I liked her then, because she didn't talk. She looked longer than I did, I had to drag her away. By the time we left, the window was covered with our fingerprints. German was always a hard quince of a language for me.

Ever since I had seen the nut, I asked Tereza every day whether she had been to the doctor about it. She twisted her rings and looked at them as if they had the answer. She shook her head, swore, and stopped eating. Her face grew rigid. One Monday she said: Yes. I asked: When? Tereza said: I went to a doctor's house yesterday. It's a fatty cyst, not what you think.

I didn't believe her and looked for the fresh, moist lie in her eyes. I saw the city child in her face, selfish and quick and sly, creeping round the corners of her mouth. But Tereza pushed the next little soldier into her mouth, chewed, and made the chickens clatter and the ball fly. I thought: When you lie, you lose your appetite. Because Tereza was able to go on eating, I stopped doubting her.

If you were changed into a bird tomorrow, asked Tereza, what kind of bird would you want to be?

Tereza couldn't say, very much longer, I've come to feed the chickens. We didn't eat together very much longer.

One morning when I showed up at work, I heard a clattering. There was no one in the corridor, it was quiet. I stood outside the office with my key in my hand. I listened, the clattering was coming from inside. I flung open the door. There was someone sitting at my desk. He was playing with the chicken-torture. I knew him by sight, he was called the programmer. He was laughing his head off. I snatched the chicken-torture away from him. He said: Visitors who come at this hour should knock on the door before stepping inside. It wasn't that I had come late, but that I had already been sacked. After I had slammed the door, I saw all my belongings out in the corridor: soap and towel, Tereza's immersion heater and pot. In the pot two spoons, two knives, coffee and sugar, and two cups. In one of the cups, an eraser. In the other, a pair of nail-clippers. I went to look for Tereza, stood around her office, laid my belongings out on her empty table. I waited awhile. The air was bad, everyone was walking back and forth. They were busying themselves in that tiny room, that thimble full of people. They stared at me out of the corners of their eyes. No one asked me why I was crying. The phone rang; someone answered it and said: Yes, she's here. He sent me to the head of personnel, who gave me a form to sign. I read it and said: No. He gave me a sleepy look. I asked: Why? He broke a biscuit in two. A couple of white crumbs fell on his dark jacket. I don't know what else came to my mind. But I shouted all the louder. I swore for the first time in my life, because I had been sacked.

Tereza didn't show up at her office that morning.

The sky was bare. A warm wind pulled me by the hair through the factory yard. I couldn't feel my legs at all. Cleanliness is next to godliness, I thought, I won't go to Heaven dirty. I wanted to be dirty just to spite Captain Pjele's Heaven, but nevertheless since that time I had started to change my underwear more often.

Three times I went back, retracing my steps, to Tereza's office, opened and shut the door without a word. My things were still all on the table. I let my tears run down my ears, my chin. My lips burned with salt, my neck was wet.

On the pavement beneath the slogan I saw my shoes shuffling where others were walking. Their hands were carrying tin sheep or fluttering pieces of paper. I saw them next to me, far away. Only the hair on their heads seemed close to me, and bigger than their shirts and dresses.

I wasn't even thinking of myself anymore, that's how frightened I was for Tereza. I swore for the second time.

All that time she was sitting in the manager's office. He had intercepted her at the factory gate and didn't let her go until three hours later, when I finally walked out the gate, after being officially dismissed. She was to join the Party that very day and turn her back on me. After three hours she said: Okay.

In the session that afternoon, Tereza had to sit in the first row directly in front of the red tablecloth of the Presidium. After the introduction. Tereza's father was honored. Then she was presented by the chairman of the session. She was invited to stand up and step forward so that everyone could see the newest member before she joined. Tereza stood up and turned to face the auditorium. Chairs creaked, people craned their necks. Tereza sensed what they were looking at: Her legs.

I bowed, as if I were a performer, Tereza said later. A few people laughed, a few even applauded. Then I started to swear. The laughing and applause quickly stopped as they noticed that no one on the Presidium platform was applauding. They felt they'd walked into a trap and hid their hands.

Why don't you all stand on your heads and see how many flies you can catch with your assholes? said Tereza. Someone in the front row put his hands on his thighs. He had been sitting on them, and they were as red as the tablecloth. So were his ears, even though he hadn't been sitting on those, said Tereza. He opened his yap, drew breath, and flexed his fingers. The man next to him, a skinny guy with long legs, gave her a kick on the ankle to get her to shut up and sit down, said Tereza. Tereza moved her foot away and said: Whoever has the most flies can be Chairman, unless you have a better idea.

My voice stayed calm, said Tereza. I smiled. I'm sure at first they thought I was going to thank them for their praise of my father. Afterward they all stared like owls, their eyes whiter than the walls of the auditorium.

One Wednesday Kurt came into the city unexpectedly. In spite of the summer day I was sitting in my room, because being among people made me cry so easily. Because I had stood in the middle of the tram in order to be able to yell. Because I had run out of the shop, so as not to have to kick and bite people.

171

Kurt brought Frau Margit some flowers for the first time, probably because he was visiting in the middle of the week. They were wildflowers, red corn-poppies and white flowering nettles. They were already wilted from the journey. They'll freshen up once they're put in water, said Frau Margit.

The flowers turned out not to be necessary. Frau Margit had mellowed since my dismissal. She stroked me, but that only made me shudder. I couldn't bear it, but I couldn't push her hand away, either. Her Jesus stared at me as well when she said: You have to pray, my child. God understands everything. I talked about Captain Pjele, and she talked about God. I was afraid my hands might fly up and smack her face.

Someone did come one time, said Frau Margit, and asked me questions about you. He smelled of sweat. She thought he was a *kanod,* a fucker. God, she said, there are so many of them, how can you tell them apart? The man had shown her his I.D., without her glasses on she hadn't been able to read what was on it. He was in the room before she could say anything. He asked her all sorts of things, Frau Margit said. It was clear from his questions that he hadn't come out of love.

She pays her rent and goes to work, that's all I know, Frau Margit had said to this man. Then she had raised her hand. I swear it, she had said, pointing to Jesus: Not a word of this is a lie, as He is my witness.

That happened in the spring, said Frau Margit. I'm only telling you now because he went away and hasn't been back since. When he left, he excused himself and kissed my hand. He was a gentleman, but he did smell of sweat.

Since then she had often prayed for me. God listens to me, she said, He knows I don't do it for everyone. But you should at least pray a little bit yourself.

Kurt came unexpectedly because Edgar and Georg had called him at the slaughterhouse to say that they'd been dismissed. They phoned your factory as well, said Kurt. Some programmer told them you'd been absent so many times that they'd had to let you go. They wanted to talk to Tereza, but then the man hung up on them.

Kurt had had a toothache the whole night. His hair was all over the place. There isn't a dentist in the village, he said, everyone just goes to the cobbler's. The cobbler has a chair with a board that comes down in front of your stomach. You sit in that, and the cobbler ties a bit of stout thread around your tooth. He ties the other end in a knot around the handle of the door to his workshop. Then he kicks the door shut. The thread pulls the tooth out of your mouth. It costs forty lei, the same as for a pair of half-soles, Kurt said.

Tereza wasn't dismissed after the Party meeting. She was transferred to a different factory.

Kurt said: She's childish, not political. Her father's very grown-up, so she can go on being childish. The corners of his eyes were redder than his hair; his mouth was wet.

My father was grown-up too, I said, after all, he served in the SS, didn't he? He would have cast monuments and put them up all over the country too. He would have marched off whenever they asked. The fact that he was of no more use politically after the war, that's not what he regretted. He had just marched off in the wrong direction, that's all.

Anyone can be used as an informer, said Kurt, no matter whether they served Antonescu or Hitler. The scars on his thumbs made him look to me like the devil's child. A couple of years after Hitler, and they were all crying their hearts out over Stalin, he said. And since then they've been helping Ceauşescu make graveyards. These little informers aren't after high office in the Party. They can be used without the slightest embarrassment. Party members can object if they're asked to be informers. They're better equipped to defend themselves.

If they want to, I said. I hated his dirty fingernails, because they distrusted Tereza. I hated his wrily twisted chin, because it half-convinced me. I hated the loose button on his shirt, because it was hanging by a thread and ripe for ripping off.

How much does a person have to do to become as political as you are? I asked. I tore off the loose button, pulled out the thread, and stuck it in my mouth. Kurt struck at my hand but missed.

You say you're being meticulous, but you're really just suspicious, I said with the thread on my tongue and the button in my hand, and still you allow Tereza to keep your photographs. So what? said Kurt, nothing will happen to her if they find them.

You think that if you don't trust anyone, you'll become invisible, I said. Kurt looked at the picture of the newly dead woman, her hoopskirt and her parasol. No, he said. Pjele won't take his eyes off us now. I bit off the thread and swallowed it: Has anyone ever chosen his own father? Kurt held his head in his hands. There are people who no longer know their own fathers, he said. I asked: Who? His fingers drummed on the empty table. They sounded like the chicken-torture. On the wood, each pair of fingers made a different sound.

I thought to myself: We know one another so well that we depend on each other. But it would have been so easy for us to have different friends, if Lola hadn't died in the closet.

Go to the dentist, I said. You're envious because we don't have anyone who can help us. He said: Now you're becoming childish, too.

Then he held his hand out like a child. But I stuck the button in my mouth: Leave it with me, you'll only lose it. The button rattled against my teeth. Where is the chicken-torture? asked Kurt.

I wrote to Mother to say I'd been dismissed. The letter reached her the next day. And by the day after that I already had her reply:

I heard about it in the village. I'm coming into town on Friday, on the early train.

I wrote back:

I can't be at the station that early. I'll meet you by the fountain at ten.

Letters had never traveled that quickly.

• • •

Mother had been in the city since early morning. We met at the fountain. She had two empty baskets hanging from her arms and a full bag at her feet. She kissed me in front of the fountain without putting her baskets down. I've done all my shopping, she said, all I need now are preserving jars.

I took the heavy bag. We went into the shop. We didn't speak to each other. If I had been carrying one of the two identical baskets, we might have looked to strangers like mother and daughter. As it was, though, people kept passing between us—we left enough space.

In the shop, Mother asked for fifteen preserving jars for cucumbers, peppers, and beets. How are you going to carry that many? I asked. No one's going to keep you, she said, no factory and no man. The whole village knows you've been fired.

I'll carry the vegetable jars and the bag, you carry the fruit jars, said Mother. And she asked for a further seventeen jars for plums, apples, peaches, and quinces. Mother had three wrinkles across her brow as she added up the fruit and vegetables. As she counted them, she had to go through all her garden beds and fruit trees in her head, so as not to forget any. All the jars that the salesclerk placed on the counter were identical.

But they're all the same anyway, I said. The clerk wrapped them up. Of course they're all the same, said my mother, but is there any law against my saying what they're to be used for? I have to include Grandmother too, she said, because in winter, when we'll be eating what's been put up, she'll be at home. You're not coming home, are you? In the train people were saying you're three months pregnant. They didn't see me, I was sitting behind them. But the people next to me heard as well, and they looked at the floor. I just wanted to crawl under the seat.

We went to the cashier. Mother spat on her thumb and forefinger and paid. Stare all you like, she said, hard work makes rough hands.

Mother put the baskets on the floor, spread her legs, stuck out her behind, and packed up the jars. Have you ever in your life thought about what it's like being a mother and having to be ashamed?

I screamed at her: If you don't shut up, you'll never see me again—not one more word.

Mother swallowed. She said quietly: What time is it?

On her wrist she had one of my father's dead wrist-watches. Why do you wear it, I asked, if it doesn't work? Nobody can see that, she said, and you have one too. Mine works, I said, otherwise I wouldn't be wearing it. If I wear a watch, it makes me feel more secure, she said, even if it's not working. Then why ask me what time it is? I said.

Because that's all I can talk to you about, said Mother.

Frau Margit had said: *Nincs lóvé nincs muzsika*—No money, no music—but what can be done, if you don't have any money now for the rent? I can hold off for two months, God will help you, and then I won't be left alone. It's not easy to

177

find a German or Hungarian girl, and I'm not having anything else in my house. You're Catholic by birth at least, and one day you'll start praying again. God has time enough, more than we do. God can see us even as we're being born. But it takes us a long time to be able to see Him. I didn't pray either when I was young. I can understand you not wanting to go back to the country, said Frau Margit, only clods live there. In Pest, if someone didn't know how to behave, we used to say: You're just a peasant.

Frau Margit was going to buy fresh cheese at the market. Very expensive, she said. I broke off a little crumb of it to taste. The peasant woman screamed at me: With those dirty hands. I wash my hands more often in a day than she does in a month. The cheese was as sour as vinegar.

I've heard, said Frau Margit, that many peasants put flour in their cheese. I know it's sinful to say so before God, but He knows it Himself, peasants were never decent people.

Frau Margit will stroke my head as interest due on my late rent, I told Tereza. She thinks she's entitled to do that. If she can't get her rent, she wants feelings. If I can find some money quickly, she won't get her hands on my head.

Tereza found me some German lessons. Three times a week I was to teach a couple of boys at their home. Their father was a foreman in the fur factory. The mother was a housewife. She is an orphan, said Tereza. The boys are a little slow. The father makes a lot of money, and that's about all you need to know.

Tereza had met the fur man and his children in the thermal baths. The children are quite attached, said Tereza. When she went off to get dressed, the father said: Come on, we're going home too.

But then he sent the children back out of the changing cabin and into the pool again. He slipped into Tereza's changing cabin in his wet trunks. He was breathing hard and grabbed at Tereza's breasts. She pushed him out. She couldn't lock the door, the bolt was missing. He stayed outside the cabin, Tereza could see his toes under the door. I didn't think you'd want to, he said. I didn't really mean it anyway, I've never cheated on my wife.

Come here, he shouted. Tereza heard the children's wet feet pattering along the tiles. When she got out of her cabin, the fur man was already fully dressed. He said: Won't you wait for us? The children haven't done anything to you, they'll be ready soon.

I heard screaming on the stairs. It came from the fourth floor, where my German lessons were going to be. When I got there I couldn't knock, the door was off its hinges. It was on the landing, propped against the wall. Smoke was streaming out of the apartment.

The fur man was slobbering, so all he could do was stammer. He stank of drink. He said: It's always good to know

German, you never know what will happen. His eyes were like the bulging white sacs on a frog. The woman was peering through the smoke toward the open window. The smoke wrapped her up before it drifted like a blanket out into the trees. There was no breeze that afternoon, and the smoke just hung in the old poplars.

The younger child was clutching a dishcloth and crying. The older one had laid its head on the table.

The Germans are a proud race, said the fur man, we Romanians are a pack of damned dogs. Cowards through and through, you can tell by the suicides. Everyone dangling from ropes, no one with the balls to shoot himself. Your Hitler didn't trust us an inch. Climb back inside your mother, screamed his wife. The fur man yanked at the cupboard: That's a good idea, but where is she?

There were bread pellets on the kitchen floor. The children had been shooting them at each other before the argument broke out.

The fur man stuck a cigarette in the corner of his mouth. His hand shook, and his head; his lighter flame couldn't find the cigarette. He dropped the cigarette on the floor. He looked at it a long time, held the lighter at a slant, and burned his thumb. He didn't notice. He bent down; his arm wasn't long enough. The flame shriveled back into the lighter. He looked at his two children. They made no move to help him. Barely avoiding the cigarette, he staggered out onto the landing.

In the stairwell the door hit the banister. There was a crash, and I ran out to look. The fur man was lying at the top of the stairs, pinned under the door. He crept out from under it and left the door where it was. With blood pouring from his nose, he dragged himself down the stairs.

He was trying to carry the door down to the street, I said when I got back to the kitchen, but he's gone now.

He tore the door off its hinges in a rage, said the younger child, then he started hitting Mother. She ran away and locked herself up in her room. He sat down at the kitchen table and drank schnapps. I went to call Mother from her room, because he had calmed down. She was going to make us some pancakes. The oil was hot. He poured the schnapps onto the fire and into the hot oil. He said he wanted to set us on fire. The flame flew up, it almost burned Mother's face. Then the kitchen cupboard caught fire. We quickly put it out, said the child.

She's come for your first lesson and walks smack into this madness, the woman said to the child. She shuffled over to the table and collapsed onto a chair.

I said: It doesn't matter. But it did matter, like all the things I could neither endure nor do anything about. And as if she were an old friend of mine, I started to stroke the woman's hair. She disappeared under my hand. She was consuming herself in her tightly tied love, of which nothing remained but two children, the smell of smoke, and a front door off its hinges. And a stranger's hand in her hair.

The woman sobbed, I could feel her heart-beast slipping out of her belly into my hand. It jumped here and there as I stroked her, only faster.

When it gets dark he'll be back, said the older child.

The woman had short hair. I could see her scalp. And in

the poplars, where the smoke had settled, I could see a young woman leaving an orphanage. I knew where in the city it was. I knew the monument outside the fence. The iron mother on the plinth and the iron child tugging at her skirt had been cast by Tereza's father. Behind the monument was a brown door. It was too late for the woman to go back inside. Behind that door, her body would have been too long for a child's cot. She had been written off by the orphans as well as by the years outside, the years that wanted love in the furry nest of a man. The bedcovers, sofa cushions, carpets, and slippers in her house were all fur, the cushions on the kitchen chairs, even the potholders.

The woman looked at her two children and said: What can you do, some children are poor because they don't have parents, others because they do.

The child goes into her room to cry. She shuts the door, lowers the blinds, and turns on the light. She stands in front of the dressing-table mirror, in which no one has ever made herself up. It has two wings you can open and shut. It's a window in which you can see yourself crying in triplicate. This makes her self-pity three times as great as it was out in the courtyard. The sun can't come in. It doesn't have any pity, because it has to stand up in the sky without any legs.

As they cry, her eyes see a poor nobody in the mirror. The back of her head, her ears, and her shoulders are all crying too. Two arms' lengths away from the mirror, even her toes are crying. When the room is shuttered up, it becomes as deep as the snow in winter. Snow burns her cheeks just like crying.

The coffee mill ground loudly, I could feel it in my teeth. The match hissed in front of the woman's mouth. The flame quickly devoured the wood and burned her fingers as the gas ring started to flicker. The tap was wide open. Then a gray jet of steam shot out of the coffee pot. The woman threw in some coffee. It spilled over the lip like black earth.

The younger child held the dishcloth under the cold water, folded it, and laid it on his forehead.

The woman and I drank coffee, the porcelain deer looked on from the mantelpiece. After her second sip, her knee bumped into mine under the table. She apologized, although earlier I'd been stroking her. The smoke had moved on, the stink stayed behind. I wished I hadn't been where my hand was holding the coffee cup.

Go down and play in the sand, said the woman, go on. It sounded like: Bury yourselves in the sand and never come back.

The coffee was as thick as ink, the grounds trickled into my mouth when I picked up the cup. There were two coffee stains on my lap. The coffee tasted of strife.

I slumped in the chair and listened to the quick steps of the children running down the stairs. I searched under the chair for my pity for the woman. The leaf-pattern on my dress went down to my ankles. My back was hunched against the chair, but the front of me between my elbows was something lifeless with two coffee stains on its lap.

By the time the children's clatter had died down in the stairwell, I had become someone who keeps company with misery, to make sure it stays put.

Together we got the door back on its hinges. She was strong, thinking only of the door. But I was thinking of her: That I would leave, while she would be left alone behind that door.

She brought a wet dishcloth from the kitchen and wiped her husband's blood off the door.

On my way home, I was carrying a nutria fur cap in my hand, and a whole sunset on my head. Frau Margit wore only headscarves, no fur caps. Hats and furs make a woman proud, she said, and God doesn't like a proud woman.

Slowly I walked across the bridge; even the river smelled of smoke. I thought of the stones, and it was as if the thought were not inside my head. It was outside, passing by. It could, if it liked, pass me quickly or slowly, like the rails of the bridge. Before I got to the end of the bridge, I wanted to see whether the river was lying on its front or its back. The water lay smoothly between the banks, and I thought: I don't need fur hats, I just need money so that Frau Margit won't stroke me.

When I got to the courtyard, Frau Grauberg's grandson was sitting on the stairs. Herr Feyerabend was brushing his shoes outside the door. The grandson was playing streetcar all by himself. When he sat down he was a passenger. When he stood up he was a ticket inspector. He said: Tickets, please. He pulled the ticket out of his other hand. The left hand was the passenger, the right the ticket inspector.

Herr Feyerabend said: If you come over here, I'll be your passenger. I'd rather be everything at once, said the boy, then I'll know who hasn't bought his ticket.

How is Elsa? I asked. Herr Feyerabend looked at the fur hat in my hand: Where have you been? You smell of smoke.

Before I could reply, he stuck his brush inside one shoe and got up to go. The boy put his arm out and said: No one is allowed to change cars, stay where you are. Without a word, Herr Feyerabend raised the boy's arm the way you lift a barrier. He gripped it too hard. You could see the fingermarks on the boy's arm as Herr Feyerabend walked down the steps into the boxwood garden.

When we lost our jobs Edgar had said: Now we've reached the end of the line. Georg shook his head: No, this is only the second-to-last stop, the last one is out of the country. Edgar and Kurt nodded. I was shocked at how little that surprised me. I merely nodded and didn't think anything of it. It seemed almost automatic, the way we finally allowed that phrase to come into our midst.

I hid the fur hat right at the back of my wardrobe. Maybe it'll look better in winter than it does now, I thought to myself. Tereza had tried it on and said: It reeks of rotten leaves. I didn't know whether she meant the hat on her head, because just before she had been showing me her nut. She did up her blouse and looked at the hat in the mirror. She was angry with me because I had said the nut had been smaller two weeks before. She wanted me to lie to her. I wanted her to go to the doctor. I'll go with you, I said. She was frightened and raised her eyebrows; the feeling of the itchy fur on her forehead disgusted her. Tereza tore the hat off and sniffed it. I'm not a child, she said.

That night I played with the chicken-torture for a long time. The beak of the red chicken no longer reached down to the board. The chicken swung its head from side to side, as if it were dizzy. It couldn't peck. The thread that ran through its belly to pull its head up and down had gotten tangled. The light fell on my arm, it didn't fall on the coffee stains in my lap. The shiny red chicken was skinny and rigid, like a weathercock: a weather-chicken, I thought. Even though it couldn't peck, it didn't look sick, it looked well nourished and bent on flying.

Frau Margit knocked on the door and said: That thing's rattling so much, I can't pray.

Captain Pjele said: You're living off private lessons, subversive activity, and common prostitution. All of which is illegal. Captain Pjele sat at his large, polished desk, and I was at a small, bare sinner's desk by the opposite wall. I saw two white ankles under his desk. And on his head a bald spot as damp and vaulted as the roof of my mouth. My tongue curled upward. His Romanian language calls the roof of the mouth the mouth-heaven. I imagined his bald head on a sawdust pillow in a coffin, and the ankles under a funeral shroud.

And apart from that, how are you? asked Captain Pjele. There was no hatred in his features. I knew I had to be careful, because his viciousness always struck from behind, when his expression was placid. I'm lucky I've got you, I said. I'm whatever way you want me to be. That's your job, isn't it?

Your mother wants to emigrate, said Captain Pjele, it says so here. He waved a piece of paper in front of me. It had handwriting on it, but I didn't think it was my mother's. I said: She may want to, but I don't.

That same day I wrote Mother asking if it was her writing. The letter never reached her.

A week later Captain Pjele told Edgar and Georg that they were living off subversive activities and parasitism. All of which was illegal. Everyone in the country knows how to read and write. They can all write poems, if they want to, and they don't have to form subversive organizations to do so. Our art is made by the people, we don't need a band of antisocial elements to do it for us. Since you write in German, why don't you go to Germany? Maybe you'll feel at home in that mire. I thought you had all come to your senses.

Captain Pjele pulled out one of Georg's hairs. He held it under his desk lamp and laughed. A bit frizzy from the sun, like a dog's, he said. But nothing a spell in the shade won't fix. Down in the cells it's nice and cool.

You can go now, said Captain Pjele. The dog Pjele was in front of the door. Would you call your dog? asked Edgar. Captain Pjele said: What for, he's sitting quietly by the door.

The dog Pjele growled. He didn't leap. He scratched Georg's shoes and ripped through Edgar's trouser cuffs. When Edgar and Georg were outside in the corridor, they heard a voice inside calling: Pjele, Pjele. It wasn't the Captain's voice, said Edgar. Maybe it was the dog, calling the Captain.

Georg rubbed his finger back and forth against his teeth. It made a squeak. We laughed. That's how you do it, Georg said, if you're arrested without a toothbrush.

I had three German lessons with the fur man's children: *Die Mutter ist gut. Der Baum ist grün. Das Wasser fliesst.* The mother is good. The tree is green. The water flows.

The children wouldn't repeat: The sand is heavy. Only: The sand is nice. They wouldn't say: The burning sun. Only: The shining sun. How do you say prize worker in German? they asked. How do you say hunter? How do you say Youth Pioneer?

The quince is ripe, I said, and thought of Tereza's nanny, and German as a hard quince of a language. The quince is furry, I said. The quince is wormy.

I wonder what I smelled like to these children.

We don't like quinces, said the younger one. What about fur? I asked—*der Pelz.* Such a short word, said the older one.

How about *das Fell,* I said. That's just as short, said the child.

The fourth time I came, the children's mother was standing on the street in front of the apartment house with a broom in her hand. I saw her from a long way off. She wasn't sweeping, she was standing and resting her elbow on the broomhandle. As I approached, she began to sweep. She didn't look at me until I said hello. There was a parcel wrapped in newspaper on the stairs.

Things are bad at the factory, she said, we can't afford the lessons anymore. She propped the broom against the wall, picked up the parcel, and gave it to me. A mink cushion and real lambskin gloves, she whispered.

My arms sagged, I couldn't raise a hand. Why are you sweeping here? I asked, the poplars are over there. Yes, she said, but the dust is here.

The broomhandle made a shadow on the wall just as Father's hoe did in the garden when the child wished that the milk thistles could live out the summer.

The woman put the parcel down on the steps and set off after me: Wait, I'll tell you something. Someone has been here and said bad things about you. I don't believe a word of it, but we can't have that sort of thing in our house. You have to understand, the children are still too young for all that.

The piece of paper that Captain Pjele waved in front of me did have Mother's writing on it. At eight in the morning, Mother had been called in by the village policeman. He dictated and she wrote. The policeman kept Mother locked in his office for ten hours. She sat down by the window. She didn't dare to open it. Each time someone passed, she rapped on the glass. No one in the street looked up. People know they're not allowed to look up there, said Mother. I wouldn't have looked up myself, because there's nothing you can do about it anyway.

I was so bored, said Mother, that I started dusting the office. I found a rag next to the cupboard. Better than just sitting and thinking about Grandmother, I thought to myself. I heard the church bells ringing, and then the key turned. It was six in the evening. The policeman switched the light on. He didn't notice I'd cleaned everything. I was too scared to tell him. I'm sorry now I didn't, it would have made him happy. A young man all on his own in the village, no one lifting a finger to help him.

He was very helpful to me. I agree with the things he told me to write. I couldn't have put it so well myself. I'm sure there are a lot of mistakes. I don't have much practice at writing. Anyway, it'll be clear enough, he couldn't have sent it on to the passport office otherwise.

The bed was covered with panties. Seventy pair, said the seamstress. A mountain of crystal was standing on the table. I'm going to Budapest, she said, why aren't you living at home now that you're without a job? It isn't home to me anymore, I said. The seamstress was making herself a bathrobe for the journey.

I won't be in my room during the day, only first thing in

the morning and at night. This time I'm staying a week. Someone who loses her mind like your grandmother can't be without feelings, she said. You ought to go home, if only for her sake. She put on the bathrobe. A pin pricked her in the neck. I pulled it out and said: You're afraid your children will leave you when they grow up. They'll do exactly what you're accusing me of.

A big hood was tacked on with the pins. I pushed my arm into it up to the elbow. She turned to me and said: The heart of any robe is the hood. You can cry without a handkerchief, I tried it yesterday. The hood slipped over my face and wiped my tears away, I didn't have to do anything myself. I pushed my finger into the tip of the hood and asked: Why were you crying?

She took off the robe before I could get my finger out of the hood. My sister and her husband fled the day before yesterday. Maybe they made it, the cards had pointed to that day. But they also showed me wind and rain. Maybe it was like that at the border, here it was dry and calm.

The sewing machine slowly squeezed the hood under the needle, the bobbin tugged at the thread. What the seamstress was saying sounded as dry as the jittering of the thread through the iron workings of the sewing machine.

I hope the customs official still remembers me. I'll put on the same clothes for the trip that I had on before, we agreed on that. I prefer it, said the seamstress with a pin in her mouth, if people order what they want in advance. They can collect the stuff when I'm back. That way I won't have them hanging around my house, picking everything up and looking and not buying anything.

There were no pins left in the material. She had stuck

them into her mouth one after another, like sentences, before putting them down on the sewing machine next to her arm. The hood was attached, with double- and triple-stitching. The seamstress knotted the ends of the threads. So that they don't ravel, she said. She pushed out the tip of the hood with her scissors and draped the hood over her head. She didn't put her arms in the sleeves.

In Hungary you can buy this gnome with a long nose, she said. It wobbles its head. You give it a little push, and if you go in whichever direction the nose points when it stops, then you'll be lucky all day. It's expensive, but this time I'm going to buy one of those good-luck gnomes, she said. Her hood had fallen over her eyes: The gnome's name is Imré. It always ends up looking left or right, never straight ahead.

I opened Mother's letter. Behind her back-pain I read: They buried the barber yesterday. He'd gotten so old and senile the last few weeks, you wouldn't have recognized him anymore. Three days ago was the Birth of Mary. I sat in the yard and rested, because you're not supposed to work on a holiday. I watched the swallows gathering on the wires and thought to myself, well, summer will be over soon. Then the barber walked into the yard. He was wearing two different shoes—a slipper and a sandal. He had his chessboard under his arm and asked where Grandfather was. But he's dead, I said. Then he lifted up his chessboard and said: What am I supposed to do? There's nothing you can do, I said, the best thing for you is to go home. All right, he said, but first, I'd like to have a game with him.

He stood there looking at the swallows with me. I felt awful. Then I said: My father's gone over to your house, he's waiting for you there. And then he left.

After they'd lost their jobs, Edgar and Georg said to me: Now we're as free as dogs on the edge of town. Only Kurt was still tied, he had to guard the secret of the blood-guzzlers. Georg moved in with Kurt—temporarily, he said—in the village of the accomplices.

When Georg walks through the village, said Kurt, all the dogs bark because he's such a total stranger. But there was one way in which he wasn't a total stranger: He had started an affair with a village girl who lived next door.

With the witlessly smiling daughter of a blood-guzzler, said Kurt. The very first evening, as I was leaving the slaughterhouse, there was Georg with this blissfully ignorant girl, walking over a stubble field that had been wheat that afternoon. Both of them had grass seeds in their hair.

Georg claimed he had just gone out and flirted with the girl over the garden fence, but it was the other way around. She had already made a pass at Kurt.

She has speckled eyes, said Kurt, and rolls her hips like a ship. All you can talk about with her is pinching the tomato suckers. And her grandmother's forgotten more on that topic than this girl will ever know. She'll open her legs for anybody. This spring the policeman was out in the fields with her, as if he were simply checking to see how the beets were getting along. Edgar was certain that it was the village policeman who had put her onto Kurt and then Georg.

Ever since my dismissal, the days were dangling from a string of coincidences, swinging back and forth and knocking me down.

The dwarf lady with the grass pigtail was still sitting in Trajan Square. She cradled a green ear of corn in her arms and was talking to it. She slit it open and held a bundle of cornsilk in her hand. She brushed the cornsilk against her cheek. She ate the silk along with the milky kernels.

Everything the dwarf lady ate turned into a baby. She was thin and her belly was fat. The shift workers had pumped her up under the cover of a spring night that must have been as quiet as the woman herself was mute. The guards had been lured away by the plum trees into different streets. Either the guards had lost sight of the dwarf lady, or else they had been instructed to turn a blind eye. Maybe the time had come for the dwarf lady to die in childbirth.

The trees of the city turned yellow, first the chestnuts, then the lindens. Since my dismissal, I had seen in the pale branches only a general condition, not autumn. The bitter scent I sometimes smelled in the air was my own, not autumn. It was hard to think about plants giving up when I should be doing the same. So I looked at them without seeing them until the dwarf lady started cramming this early autumn into her mouth, the cornsilk and the milky kernels.

I met Edgar in Trajan Square. He was carrying a white canvas bag. It was half full of nuts, he gave them to me. They're supposed to be good for the nerves, he said sardonically. I put a handful of nuts in the dwarf lady's lap. She took one, put it in her mouth, and tried to bite it open. Then she spat it out again like a ball. The nut trundled over the ground. Then the dwarf lady took all the nuts, one after another, and sent them all spinning over the stones. The passersby laughed. The dwarf lady's eyes were round and earnest.

Edgar took a fist-sized stone that was lying next to a trash can. You need to crack them open, he said to the dwarf lady, there's something inside that you can eat. He banged on the nut. The dwarf lady covered her eyes and shook her head.

Edgar pushed the cracked nut to the side of the pavement with his shoe and tossed his stone into the rubbish.

The child puts a nut in her father's left hand and another in his right. She always imagines them as two heads: the heads of Father and Mother, the heads of Grandfather and the barber, the head of the devil's child and her own head. Her father laces his fingers together.

There is a crack.

Stop that, says the singing grandmother, I feel it in my brain.

The child leaves her singing grandmother out of the game, because her brain has already started to crack.

When Father opens his hands, the child looks to see whose head has survived and whose is in pieces.

．．．

We walked from Trajan Square down the narrow little alley that was curved like a sickle. Edgar was walking too fast, he had made the dwarf lady cry by cracking open the nut. He was thinking about her.

You can't do it, said Edgar, I won't let you. Listen, I have to go back tonight. I don't have any place to sleep. You have to promise not to do it. I didn't say a word. Edgar stopped and yelled: Did you hear me? A cat climbed up a tree. I said: See that? She has white socks on.

You're not alone in this, said Edgar. You can't do anything we haven't all agreed on. If they catch you, we're all guilty. And then there's nothing to be done. Edgar stumbled over a root that lay curled under the asphalt like an arm.

I was sick of his voice. I laughed, not because he'd stumbled, but in rage. When you were all away at school, I was living a life too. You say you speak for everyone, but Georg and Kurt were both in favor.

Eat your nuts, said Edgar, they'll make you smarter.

Edgar lived in the country with his parents. They didn't hold his dismissal against him. That's the way it always was, said Edgar's father. Your grandfather couldn't become a station-master in the Hungarian years because he refused to let them Magyarize his name. He stayed on laying track, and building the viaduct in the valley. Some idiot who wrote his name with an sz was given the uniform and warmed his behind on a leather chair. And when the train whistled, he leapt up and hopped out the door with his dirty little flag. He puffed out his chest to make himself as imposing as he could. Your grandfather couldn't look at him without laughing.

When the evening train had made its way down the tracks with Edgar on board, I looked at the stones between the railroad ties. They were no bigger than nuts. Further on, the tracks ran through oily grass. The sky extended farther than they did. I walked slowly in the direction the train had gone, until the platform came to an end. Then I turned back.

I stood in front of the main station clock and watched. People went rushing by with baskets and bags, the second hand jumped, the buses nearly scraped their sides going around the corner. Then I noticed I was carrying only my handbag and had forgotten Edgar's nuts on the bench. I went back down the platform. The next train was already standing by. The bench was empty.

There was only one path beneath my feet, the path that led to the telephone booth.

I could hear the phone ring twice, then I gave a made-up name. Tereza's father believed me and called her to the phone.

197

Tereza came into town and met me by the pollarded willow with three trunks that grew a long way down the riverbank. I showed her the preserving jar and the paintbrush in my handbag.

I'll show you the house, said Tereza, but I'm not getting involved in this. I'll wait for you around the corner. I had crapped in the preserving jar and had decided to daub it on Captain Pjele's house. I wanted to write prick or pig on the wall below the tall windows. Some short word that wouldn't take long to write.

A different name was listed at the house where Captain Pjele was supposed to be living. But Tereza knew where the factory manager lived, so we went there instead.

There was still light behind the curtains there. Tereza and I waited. It was almost midnight, we paced back and forth. Tereza's bracelets jangled and I said: Take them off. Then the wind was blowing against all sorts of black things. I saw people where in fact there were only bushes. I saw faces in parked cars that had only empty seats in them. Leaves fell on the path where there were no trees. Our feet shuffled and stumbled. Tereza said: Your shoes are no good.

The moon was a crescent. It'll be brighter tomorrow, said Tereza, it's waxing, its hump is on the right. The streetlamp is directly in front of the house. That sort of house is always lit up. That's good, because you can see the wall; but they can see us too.

I looked for the right spot between the two middle windows. I put the paintbrush in my jacket pocket, unscrewed the lid of the jar, and gave it to Tereza. I left my handbag open.

It reeks, as if they'd already caught you, said Tereza. She went around the corner with the lid.

By the time I turned the corner, there was no one there. I went from fence to fence, from gate to gate, from tree to tree. Not until the very end of the street did someone step out from a tree trunk, as if through a door. I had to look three times before it became Tereza. I smelled her perfume.

Come on, she said, taking me by the arm, my God, it took you long enough, what did you write? I said: Nothing. I just left the jar outside the front door.

Tereza cackled with laughter like a chicken. Her long, pale throat stretched out next to me, as if her legs began at her shoulders. It still reeks, said Tereza, you got it all over you. Where's the lid? I asked. At the foot of the tree where I was waiting, she said.

We threw the paintbrush off the bridge into the river. The water was black and as still as the waiting in our heads. We held our breath and heard no splash. I was sure the paintbrush hadn't reached the water. I took a breath and had to cough because the hairs of the brush tickled my throat. I saw the crescent moon and was sure that the brush was dangling in the air and painting a dark sphere over the city—the black-ribbed night.

. . .

Edgar was back in town. We sat in the bodega for hours waiting for Georg. He didn't show. Two policemen did, and they went from table to table. The tin-sheep and wooden-melon proletariat produced their papers and named their places of work.

The madman with the white beard plucked at the sleeve of one of the policemen, opened up his folded handkerchief, and said: professor of philosophy. One of the waiters threw him out. I'll bring charges against you, young man, he screamed, you and that policeman, but the sheep are eating. The sheep will get you, make no mistake. Tonight a star will fall, and the sheep will eat you off your pillows like grass.

Edgar showed his papers. Teacher at the High School for Light Industry, the one next to the museum, he said. I held out my papers and said Translator, giving the name of the factory from which I'd been dismissed. My face was burning, and I caught the eye of the young policeman so he wouldn't notice the pounding in my temples. He leafed through our papers and handed them back. Knock on wood, said Edgar.

He looked at his watch, he had to catch his train. I stayed sitting at the table and saw his hand brushing the empty seat of the chair next to him as he got up to go. He pushed the chair up against the table and said: Georg won't be showing up anymore today.

The shift workers got louder after Edgar left. Glasses clinked and smoke swirled through the air. Chairs scraped, feet shuffled. The policemen had gone. I drank another beer, though every mouthful of it tasted like gallbladder tea.

A fat man with red cheeks pulled the waitress onto his lap. She laughed. A toothless man dunked his sausage in mustard and shoved it into her mouth. She bit into it and, as she chewed, wiped the mustard off her chin with her bare forearm.

These men and their cravings away from home, between shifts—how they pant for love one minute and pour scorn on it the next. The same ones who followed Lola into the scruffy park or pumped up the belly of the dwarf lady on quiet nights in the square. Who sold Jesus by the sackful and drank up the money. Who brought veal kidneys or scraps of parquet home to their wives. And who gave their children or lovers dust-gray rabbits to play with. Georg too was one of them, with his chicken-torture; so was the girl next door with the speckled eyes, the accomplice who Kurt said laughed like a shambling beast. But Kurt himself was no different, with his bunches of wildflowers for Frau Margit, with their heads drooping from the long hot train ride. Also the seamstress, taking money for fates and fortunes and draping golden hearts around her children's necks. And the fur man's wife with her nutria cap. And Edgar and his nuts. But I belonged to them, too, with my Hungarian sweets for Frau Margit. And with the man I didn't miss when he was dead. What had passed between us seemed to me as ordinary as a piece of bread—you swallow, it's gone. Just like the grassy spot in the woods. And my being the straw—legs open, eyes shut, suffering the trees and the crows' nests as they all look down on this piece of dung burning and freezing on the ground.

The madman with the white beard had come back into the bodega. He dragged himself to my table and drank the sip of beer left in Edgar's glass. Hearing him gulp it down, I thought about the dream I'd told Edgar:

A little red scooter, its motor rumbling. But it doesn't have a motor, the man riding it has to push it with his foot. He's going fast, his scarf is fluttering behind him. He must be in a room, I said, because the scooter is rolling across a parquet floor toward a section of baseboard and then vanishing into the dark gap between the parquet and the baseboard. Once both man and scooter have vanished completely, a pair of white eyes peeps out of the gap. One of the people passing by me on the parquet says: That's the crash-scooter.

Grandmother should sing forever, Mother should forever roll her strudel dough out across the table, Grandfather should always play chess, Father should always hack down the milk thistles, they should stay as they are instead of suddenly changing into who knows what. They should stay frozen, ugly as they are, the child thinks to herself, rather than turn into other people. Better to be at home in room and garden among ugly people than belong to strangers.

Two days later Kurt came into town. He gave Frau Margit a bouquet of bindweed. They stuck out their little red tongues and smelled of cake.

Kurt said: The girl next door with the speckled eyes knocked on my window last night. She was holding a little rabbit in her arms and told me that Georg had started a fight with some strangers near the station in town. He's in the hospital. Yesterday morning I was in the village, said Kurt. The policeman called to me from the other side of the street. I didn't go over to him, I stayed where I was. I stooped and picked a yellow leaf off the ground. I stuck the stem in my mouth. The policeman crossed the street, shook my hand, and invited me over to his house for a little schnapps. He was calling me by my first name, I asked him not to. He said: We'll see about that. He lives right near where we were standing. I refused his schnapps. The policeman expected me to walk on, but I didn't move, I just kept turning the leaf around and around with my mouth. He didn't have anything more to say, but he couldn't bring himself to leave, either. So as not to have to watch the leaf turning in my mouth, he bent down to tie his laces. I spat the leaf out on the ground next to his hand and walked off. He shouted something after me, probably some swearword.

Kurt and I went to the hospital. Kurt gave the porter a bottle of schnapps. He took it and said: He has a room to himself on the fourth floor. I'm telling you that, though I'm not supposed to. But I can't let you go up and see him.

On the way back through the city, Kurt said: It was Georg who gave the girl next door the little rabbit she was holding. Georg rescued it from a cat in the fields somewhere and gave it to the daughter of one of the blood-guzzlers. It's beautiful, as gray as dusty earth. It was trembling all over when Georg brought it in. The skin over its belly was so thin. I thought its insides would fall out when it jumped out of my hand.

How does she know about Georg being in the hospital? I asked. The rabbit told her, said Kurt, and he laughed.

Georg had a fractured jaw. When he was released from the hospital he said: I recognized the faces of the three thugs who did it from my student days, from the cafeteria. But just by sight; I don't know their names.

They had jostled him as soon as he got off the train. He tried to avoid them. I thought they were going to lay into me right then and there, said Georg, but they let me get a little distance from the station, because there were too many people on the platform.

Next to the bus stop, they cornered Georg between the wall and the kiosk. Fists and boots, that's all I can remember, said Georg.

A little, withered man woke Georg up. In the hospital. He stood in front of Georg's bed, took his wallet out of his jacket, put some money on the bedside table, and said: There, now we're quits. Georg flung his pillow, then his teacup at the man's head. He smiled, said Georg, with the tea dribbling down his face. He took his shitty money off the table and went. He wasn't one of the three.

The girl with the speckled eyes went into town to visit Georg in the hospital, carrying her dusty rabbit in a basket. She was allowed into his room. The rabbit had to stay downstairs with the porter. The porter fed the animal some bread. The girl gave Georg apples and cake and stroked his hair. But Georg wanted to know when she'd last seen the village policeman.

She's too stupid to lie, said Kurt, she drank a sip of Georg's tea and burst into tears. Georg yelled at her. He stuffed the cake and the apples back into her basket and showed her the door. She left the rabbit with the porter, telling him it belonged to the patient she'd just visited, who would pick it up when he left the hospital.

When Georg went out the gate ten days later, the porter knocked on the glass and pointed to the rabbit. It was sitting in a cage on the hat shelf, nibbling potato peelings. Georg shook his head and kept on going. The porter called: Don't bother coming back for him later, he's our Sunday dinner.

The court refused to hear the case against the thugs. We hadn't expected anything else.

When Georg went to court, the official already knew all about him. Captain Pjele had had ten full days to settle him. Georg said: I'd like to try anyway.

Where do you work? asked the official. It's easy enough here for people with nothing better to do to go around filing charges against persons unknown, and with no proof.

I have plenty of things to do, and I'm just out of the hospital—that's how badly I was beaten, said Georg. Then where is your doctor's certificate to say so? asked the official. I wasn't given one because the doctor was away at a wedding when I was released, said Georg.

Georg had the certificate in his pocket, but all it said was: Summer influenza with nausea.

Your sufferings, said the official, are the product of laziness, paranoia, and an overactive imagination. Take your certificate with you, you're lucky your real illness isn't mentioned on it. You think you're innocent, but no one gets beaten up without cause.

Georg spent that day in the bodega next to the station. He had bought a ticket to his parents'. Georg went out to the platform, ticket in hand, and sat down on a bench. He watched people carrying sacks and buckets up the stairs and climbing aboard the train. The doors were open, heads were lolling out of the open window all in a row. Women were eating apples, children were spitting onto the platform, men were spitting on their combs and slicking down their hair. Georg was overcome with disgust.

The doors were slammed shut. The train whistled, the wheels turned, the passengers looked back down the platform.

He didn't want, said Georg, to fall back on a freckled seamstress, who takes in sewing and ironing and who refers to her son as a failure. Who, behind her husband's back, sends the boy a little money and a lot of reproaches in the same envelope. He didn't want to go back to a retired father more concerned with his bicycle than with his son. Nor did he want to go back to Kurt in the village of the accomplices. And he didn't want to see the girl next door with her speckled eyes ever again.

I didn't want to go to Edgar's parents or to Frau Margit either, said Georg. I felt only one desire, and that was never to take another step on this earth. I went to the waiting room, exhausted and empty, showed my ticket to the station master, and lay down on a bench. I fell asleep at once, like a piece of abandoned luggage. Until it got light and a policeman with a stick made his rounds, I slept deeply. By the time I left, the other people in the waiting room were talking about morning trains. They all had somewhere to go.

Georg woke up and—without a word to Edgar, Kurt, or me—headed straight for the passport office.

I had no interest in letting you calm me down, said Georg, no pats on the back, no there-there coming out of your mouths. I hated you; in the state I was in, I wouldn't have been able to look at you. The mere thought of you drove me into a rage. I felt like spewing you out of my life, and myself too, because I realized how much we all depended on one another. And so, hardly knowing where I was going, I made my way to the passport office and there at the counter, like a drowning man I filled out my application to emigrate and submitted it on the spot. Quickly, before Captain Pjele could show up. All the time I was writing, I felt he was looking over my shoulder.

Georg no longer remembered what he had written.

Except that I wished I could leave the country that very day, it definitely said that. Now I feel better, he said, almost like a human being. After I handed in the application, I could hardly wait to see you.

Georg put one hand on my head, and with the other he tugged at Edgar's earlobe.

It was just your own insecurity, said Edgar, you had to outwit yourself. None of us would have tried to talk you out of leaving.

The seamstress never came back from her trip to Hungary. Who would have guessed it? said Tereza. Reading cards for others had made the seamstress herself inscrutable. Tereza was offended, she had ordered a four-leaf clover for her gold chain and hadn't had an inkling of the seamstress's intention to flee.

Now her grandmother is living in the flat and looking after the children, said Tereza. She was sitting by the sewing machine when Tereza came in, as though she had been there forever. The children called her Mother, and for a while Tereza herself wasn't sure whether the woman was not in fact the seamstress. She looks exactly like the seamstress, said Tereza, just twenty years older. It's frightening how much alike they are. The grandmother talks to the children in Hungarian; did you know the seamstress was a Hungarian? I wonder why she kept that a secret. Because we don't speak Hungarian, I said. We don't speak German either, said Tereza, and yet we know that you're German. The children still don't understand that their mother has gone. How long will they be able to go on saying, without crying: Our mother's in Vienna, she's saving up to buy a car.

The nut in Tereza's armpit had grown to the size of a plum and started to ripen, turning blue in the middle. The birch tree with the door handle in its trunk was peering into the room. Tereza was sewing herself a dress, I was supposed to be helping her. Sew the buttonholes and stitch the hems.

When I do it, the thread on the buttons gets so thick, it looks awful, said Tereza, and the hems come out crooked.

Tereza's boyfriend the doctor, whom I had only once seen in town with Tereza, worked in the Party hospital. He was working day and night shifts. He was treating Tereza's father's spine, her mother's varicose veins, and her grandmother's arteriosclerosis. He wasn't interested in examining Tereza.

All I see is sick people night and day, he said to Tereza. I've had it up to here with them. I don't want to play doctor with you too. He told her to keep going to her present doctor. When Tereza told him the other doctor's opinion, he said: Well, he ought to know, and shook his head. The other doctor's opinion—if Tereza was telling the truth and had actually been to see him—was: The lump has to reach its full size before we can cut it out.

I find it strange that the man I love won't examine me, said Tereza. But I wouldn't want him to treat me. Then I'd be like all the others whose flesh passes through his hands, I wouldn't have any more secrets.

The white porcelain hand holding Tereza's jewelry stood on the table, surrounded by scraps of material.

When we sleep together, I keep my blouse on so he doesn't see the lump. He lies on top of me and pants until he's done. Then he jumps up and smokes a cigarette, and I'm wishing he would stay and lie down with me a bit longer. We're both thinking about the lump. He says I'm being childish when I ask: Why are you in such a hurry to get up? So now I don't ask anymore, said Tereza, but that doesn't mean that it doesn't bother me anymore.

You put on the dress, said Tereza, maybe it'll fit you. You know it's much too big for me, I said.

Even if it had fit, I wouldn't have put it on. It had the nut inside it. Even when I held the dress in my hands to sew it, I imagined that I was sewing the nut onto myself. That the nut was traveling down the length of the thread and into my body.

As I was sewing the buttonholes, Tereza decided she didn't like the dress anymore.

Tereza's father had gone to the south of the country for two weeks to cast a monument. That's how I was able to visit her at home. Tereza's mother had joined him later, to be there for the unveiling.

Her grandmother wasn't to know about my being there. Tereza lured her into the garden till I was safely in her room. She doesn't have anything against you, said Tereza, sometimes she asks after you. A couple of years ago, she wouldn't have said a thing. But ever since her sclerosis, her tongue's a lot looser.

Mother's letter contained three hundred lei for the rent. Behind the back-pain, I read: I've sold potatoes and saved so that you won't have to do anything bad to earn money. The nights are getting cold, last night I had to light a fire for the first time. Grandmother is still sleeping outside. The tractor drivers who go out to plow at some ungodly hour usually see her at the back of the graveyard. Maybe it's calling to her, that would be good.

Yesterday the priest came to me all red in the face. I thought he might have had one too many, but he was actually red with rage. He said: God Almighty, this can't go on. Yesterday Grandmother slipped into the sacristy while the acolyte's back was turned. When the priest came to celebrate Mass, she pointed at his black surplice and white collar. You're a swallow, too, she said, I'll get changed, then we can fly away together.

The two drawers in the sacristy cupboard were empty. Grandmother had eaten all the Communion wafers. Mass was beginning. Six people had made their confessions, said the priest. They went up to the altar to take Communion and knelt there with their eyes shut. He had to perform his sacred duty. He went from one to the next with the chalice, which had only two half-eaten wafers in it. They opened their mouths to take the wafers. As always he had to say, the body of Christ. He laid the nibbled wafers on the tongues of the first two. With the next four he just said, the body of Christ, and pressed the ball of his thumb down on their tongues.

I had to apologize, wrote Mother. With all respect, said the priest, something like that I have to report to the bishop.

Georg moved in with Edgar's parents.

The girl next door with the speckled eyes seems to have vanished off the face of the earth, said Georg. The policeman dumped her. Her garden's been harvested, the grass there is growing sky-high. What was I going to do all day at Kurt's? It gets dark so early. Kurt's away at the slaughterhouse until evening. He'd come back and fry us four eggs, and we'd drink a little schnapps to help them go down. Then he'd collapse on the bed without washing his hands. When Kurt was asleep, I used to wander all over the house clutching the bottle. There were dogs barking outside, and a few night birds were shrieking. I would listen to them and finish off the bottle. When I was half-plastered, I'd open the front door and look out into the garden. A light would be on next door. During the daytime there was the withered garden between us, and I wanted nothing to do with her. But when it got dark, I wanted her. I'd lock the front door and lay the big key on the inside windowsill. I was dying to unlock the door, run straight through the garden, and bang on her window. She was waiting for me. Each night was torture. Only the big key lying on the windowsill held me back. That's how close I came to climbing back in bed with her.

If Kurt did open his mouth at supper, it was always to do with pipes and ditches and cows. And blood guzzling, of course. I couldn't swallow a thing when Kurt talked about blood guzzling while he ate. But he liked the taste of certain sentences, such as: The colder it gets, the more blood they guzzle. He'd polish off my portion too, and swab the pan with bread.

I had to get out of the house in the daytime, said Georg—anywhere, otherwise I'd have gone crazy. The village street was dead, so I headed the other way, out of the village. There wasn't any spot I hadn't been to at least three times. There was no point in wandering over the fields. The earth was wet with dew and wouldn't dry out in the cold. Everything was cut down, pulled up, sickled, and baled. Only the weeds still stood, ripening down to the roots. They scattered their seeds. I kept my lips pressed together; there were grass seeds down my neck, in my hair and my ears. They itched, and I had to scratch. There were plump cats lurking in the undergrowth. The stalks didn't rustle. The old rabbits still managed to flee. The young ones flipped over, and that was that. It wasn't my throat they were sinking their teeth into. Frozen and dirty as a mole, I just walked on by, I'll never rescue another rabbit.

It's true, said Georg, these grasses are beautiful, but when you stand in the middle and look around, the fields seem to open their jaws. The sky withdrew, the earth clung to my

213

boots. The leaves, stalks, and roots of the grasses all turned red as blood.

Edgar came into town without Georg. The night before, Georg had still been looking forward to getting out of the village at last and, instead of muck and grass, seeing asphalt and trams again. But in the morning he dawdled and couldn't get ready in time.

Georg refused to hurry. Edgar sensed that Georg wanted to miss the train. Finally, halfway to the station, he stopped and said: I'm going back, I'm not going into town with you.

His griping about being lonely at Kurt's was just an excuse, said Edgar. He's not lonely now, I'm at home all day and so are my parents. But it's impossible to talk to him. He's like a ghost.

Georg would wake up early, get dressed, and sit down by the window. When he heard the clatter of dishes and cutlery, he'd move his chair over to the table. After breakfast, he'd take it back to the window. He gazed out. There was always the same bare acacia trunk, the ditch, the bridge, muck and grass, nothing else. What time does the newspaper come? he asked. After the postman had brought it, he never gave it a look. He was waiting to hear from the passport office. When Edgar went to the village shop or out for a walk, Georg never went along. It's not worth putting my shoes on for, he said.

He's starting to get on my parents' nerves, said Edgar. Not because of the board and lodging; after all, he's paying for that, even though my parents didn't ask for any money. My mother says: He's living here with us and makes us feel we're in his way, the man has no manners.

Every day Edgar found it harder to explain to his parents that the Georg he knew was different, that he'd become obsessed because his skull was so crammed full of worries. They said: What does he have to worry about, he's getting his passport soon, isn't he?

It all began that October morning when Georg turned back halfway to the station and Edgar went into town on his own, a bad day.

On the train there was a group of men and women singing hymns. The women held lighted candles in their hands. But their singing wasn't slow and melancholy, as in church. They adjusted the rhythm to the rattling and banging of the train. They swayed from side to side. The women sang in thin, high voices, as though they were threatened, as though they were whimpering instead of screaming. Their eyes were bulging out of their heads. They waved their candles in sweeping arcs, it was scary because they could have set the whole train on fire. The other passengers whispered to each other that the singers belonged to a sect from a neighboring village. The ticket-collector didn't set foot in that carriage, the singers didn't want to be disturbed and had bribed him. Outside the fields passed by, withered, forgotten corn and black, leafless sunflower stalks. And in the middle of that barrenness, just past a bridge where there was a bit of scrub, one of the singers got up and pulled the emergency brake. He said: We have to pray here.

The train stopped, and the group got off. In the bushes, before which the group was gathering, there were some candle ends from a previous time. The sky lowered, the group sang, and the wind blew out their candles. Everyone else, still in the carriage, clustered around the windows and looked out.

Only Edgar and another man remained seated. The man was shaking, he kept clenching his hands into fists. He pounded his thighs and stared down at the floor. Suddenly he pulled off his cap and started to cry. They're waiting for me, he said to himself out loud. He pressed his cap against his face. He swore at the sect and said: All my money, thrown away.

When the sect had climbed back on board, the train slowly started moving again. The weeping man opened the window and stared at the empty tracks ahead as if his eyes could shorten the distance. He put his cap back on and sighed. The train was taking its time.

Just outside the city, the women blew out their candles and put them in their coat pockets. Their coats and the seats were spattered with drops of wax like congealed fat.

The train stopped. The men of the sect got out first, then the women. After the women, everyone else.

The weeping man got up, went to the rear of the carriage, and looked out at the platform. Then he came back, sat down in the corner, and lit a cigarette. There were three policemen on the platform. When everyone had got off, they boarded the train and pushed the man out onto the platform. His cap was knocked off as they led him away. A box of matches fell out of his jacket pocket. The man turned around twice to look at Edgar. Edgar picked up the matchbox and put it in his pocket.

He stood in front of the main station clock. There was a sharp wind. He saw the corner where Georg had been beaten up. There was a whirl of paper and dead leaves between the kiosk and the wall. Edgar walked down the street and into town. Town is all around you when you have no place to go.

Edgar went to the barber. Because there are fewer customers in the morning, said Edgar. And then he said: Because I didn't know what to do, my hair started bothering me. I wanted to be somewhere warm, I wanted to be looked after for a time by someone who didn't know anything about me.

Edgar still referred to the barber from his student days as: our barber. At that time Edgar, Kurt, and Georg all used to go in a group to the man with the wily eyes, because his insolence was better shared among the three of them. And because he stopped being mean once he started cutting hair. Then he became almost shy, or he didn't talk.

The barber shook Edgar's hand: Ah, so you're back in town. And your two redheaded pals? he asked. His face hadn't aged at all. A lot of men won't be back for haircuts until spring, he said. They'll wear caps, and drink up whatever money they save on haircuts.

The barber had a long nail on his right index finger; all

217

the others were short. He parted Edgar's hair with his finger-nail. Edgar heard the scissors snipping, watched his face get smaller and smaller as mirror after mirror kept getting farther and farther away. Edgar closed his eyes, he felt wretched.

The barber never asked how I wanted my hair, said Edgar. He was shearing me for everyone who wouldn't be back until spring. When I got out of the chair, my hair was as short as a dog's pelt.

Back then, when Edgar, Kurt, Georg, and I were still students, there were lots of things we saw in the exact same way. But bad luck fell on each of us differently, once we were scattered about the country. We remained dependent on one another. The letters with hairs in them only served to let each of us read his own fears in the handwriting of another. Each of us had to deal with his own burrs, butcher birds, blood-guzzlers, hydraulic machines—keep his eyes wide open and tightly shut at the same time.

When we lost our jobs, we realized that we were worse off without that reliable distress than when we were under its constraint. While we were failures in the eyes of the people around us whether we had work or not, we now became failures in our own eyes as well. Although we went through the whole list of justifications and found them all valid, we still felt we were failures. We were broken, sick of the rumors about the dictator's imminent death, weary of people killed trying to flee. We were moving closer and closer to obsession with flight, without even noticing it.

Failure was as normal to us as breathing. We shared it just as we shared our trust. And yet each of us quietly added something special for himself as well: an extra bit of personal failure on the side. We each had a wretched image of ourself, along with outbreaks of agonizing vanity.

Kurt's split thumb, Georg's fractured jaw, the dust-gray rabbit, the stinking glass jar in my handbag—each of us had something. And the others knew about it.

Each of us imagined how we might desert our friends by committing suicide. And we each accused the others—without ever saying so—of being the sole reason for our not going through with it. In this way, we each became self-righteous, armed with a ready silence that blamed the others for the fact that we were each still alive instead of dead.

What it took to save us was patience. We could never run out of it; if it happened to snap, it had to spring right back up again.

When Edgar crossed the square with his new haircut, he heard the patter of a dog's paws at his heels. He stopped to let a man and a dog pass him. The dog was that mutt Pjele, said Edgar. He didn't know who the man with a black hat was. The dog sniffed at Edgar's coat and growled. The man tugged at his leash. The dog strained at the leash to turn and look at him. At the next set of lights, the man and the dog were once again behind Edgar. When the lights changed, they crossed the street and went into the park. Someone must have been waiting for the dog there, because a little later the man, now unaccompanied, climbed onto the tram after Edgar.

Edgar said: I was thinking to myself, the fellow with the hat is not a human being, and I, with my stubbly pelt, am not a dog. Despite appearances.

When Georg had retraced his steps from the point halfway to the station, he came into the room out of breath. He'd probably been running. Edgar's mother asked him: Did you forget something? Georg said: Myself. He moved the chair over to the window and gazed out at the empty day.

A little before noon, the postman knocked on the door. Apart from the newspaper, he had a registered letter. Georg didn't budge. Edgar's father said: The letter's for you, you have to sign for it.

The envelope contained the decision about a passport for Georg. He took the letter up to his room, closed the door, and lay down on the bed. Edgar's parents heard him crying. Edgar's mother knocked on the door, bringing him a cup of tea. Georg sent her away, tea and all.

When the cutlery clattered downstairs, he didn't come to lunch. Edgar's father knocked on the door, bringing him a peeled apple. He left the apple without saying anything. Georg's head was hidden under a pillow.

Edgar's parents went out into the courtyard. His mother fed the ducks, his father chopped firewood. Georg picked up a pair of scissors and went over to the mirror. He hacked away at his hair.

When Edgar's parents came back in, he was sitting by the window. He looked like a half-eaten beast. Edgar's father was alarmed, but he managed to keep calm. He said: What's the point of that?

When I saw Georg the next time, I said: You can't leave looking like that, go to the barber. He said: I won't do anything for any of you when I'm in Germany. Did you hear me, I won't lift a finger for you.

Kurt, Edgar, and I looked at the bare spots where Georg had snipped his hair down to the scalp. Kurt said to Edgar: Your hair looks pretty funny too.

When the child no longer knows what to do with herself, she takes a pair of scissors up to her room. The child lowers the blinds and switches on the light. She stands in front of the dressing-table mirror and cuts her hair. The child can see herself reflected in triplicate, and her bangs come out crooked.

The child snips the crooked ends straight but then the bits next to them seem uneven. The child snips those bits even, but then the ends she cut first once again seem crooked.

Instead of bangs, the child ends up with a spiky brush above her face, and a bare forehead. The child can't help crying.

The mother smacks her and asks: Why did you do that? The child says: Because I can't stand myself.

The whole household waits for the bangs to grow

back again from that spiky brush. Most of all, the child waits.

Days pass. The bangs grow back.

But then one day the child once more doesn't know what to do with herself.

There are lots of photographs of bare winter trees and lush, leafy summer trees. The trees have snowmen or roses in front of them. And right at the front of the pictures stands a child with a smile as uneven as the brush above her face.

The matchbox from the man on the train showed a flame, crossed out, and a tree. Underneath the picture it said: Protect your forests. Edgar put the matchbox in the kitchen. A couple of days later his mother said: There are some numbers written on the inside of the box, under the matches.

There were foreign freight trains at the shunting yard, said Edgar, the man was trying to cross the border.

The numbers in the box looked like foreign phone numbers. Edgar filled the matchbox right up to the top with new matches. He laid their red heads over each other, one at a time. Then he slid the box half-shut, like a coverlet on a bed: When you get to Germany, call these numbers.

Georg pushed the lid over the matchheads. With his hacked-at hair that none of us could get used to, he already looked like a stranger. I haven't left yet, said Georg. If they don't throw me off the moving train, I'll try and call them.

．．．

We never found out whether Georg called them or not. He wasn't issued a passport at the counter. Instead, he was sent to Captain Pjele. Captain Pjele acted as though he didn't notice Georg's hacked-at hair. He said: Take a seat, please. He used the polite form of address for the first time.

Captain Pjele laid a form and a ballpoint pen on the little desk and sat down at his own big desk. He stretched his legs and pushed back his chair. Just a little signature, said Captain Pjele. Georg read the form, which stated that he wouldn't do anything detrimental to the Romanian people when he was abroad.

Georg refused to sign.

Captain Pjele pulled in his legs and stood up. He walked over to the cupboard and took out an envelope. He put the envelope on the little table. Open it, said Captain Pjele. Georg opened the envelope.

These might come in handy now, said Captain Pjele, I can write you letters too.

The envelope was full of red hairs. Not mine, said Georg, I think they were Kurt's.

Three days later, Georg got on the train. He had the matchbox in his coat pocket. He wasn't thrown off the moving train. He arrived in Germany.

Before he left he said: I won't ever write another letter,

only postcards. His first went to Edgar's parents: A winter scene, a path with gnarled trees beside a river. He thanked Edgar's parents for having let him stay with them. The card took two months to arrive. By the time it dropped into the letter box at the gate, it was already posthumous.

Two weeks earlier the postman had knocked on the door, Edgar signed for the telegram.

Early in the morning, six weeks after emigrating, Georg lay on the pavement in Frankfurt outside the transit hostel. Six floors up was an open window.

The telegram said: Death was instantaneous.

By the time the postcard with Georg's writing dropped into the letter box, Edgar, Kurt, and I had already been to the newspaper offices twice with an obituary.

The first time the editor took the sheet of paper in his hand and nodded.

The second time he screamed at us to get out. Before we left, we put the sheet of paper on his desk, next to his glasses.

The third time we didn't get past the porter.

The obituary never appeared.

Edgar's parents kept the card from Georg in their bedroom in front of the ornamental glassware in their display cabinet. The winter scene looked at them in bed. When Edgar's mother got up in the morning, she crossed the floor in her bare feet and looked through the glass at the winter scene. Edgar's father said: I'll put it away in the drawer. Get dressed. Edgar's mother got dressed, but the card remained in the display cabinet.

Edgar's mother never used the scissors that Georg had cut his hair with for dressmaking again.

After Georg's death I could no longer lie in the dark. Frau Margit said: If you sleep, it will help his soul to find peace, and besides, who's going to pay the electric bill? Even when you can't sleep, it's more restful to lie in the dark.

I could hear Frau Margit through the door. She was groaning, while she was either sleeping or lost in thought. My toes were sticking out of the end of the bed. The chicken-torture was lying on my belly. The dress on the chair looked like a drowned woman. I had to move it somewhere else. My stockings dangled like severed legs over the back of the chair.

In the dark, I found myself inside a sack. Inside the one with the belt, inside the one with the window. And inside the one that never became mine, the one with the stones.

Frau Margit said: He might have been pushed. I think I'm a good judge of character, and Georg didn't look like that type. He won't be getting up again. If it was murder God will take him by the hand. For suicide you go to Purgatory. I'll pray for him.

Kurt came across nine poems by Georg right at the back of a cupboard. Eight of them were called: Ninekiller Shrike, the Butcher Bird. The last was: Who can take a single step with his head?

Edgar had a recurring dream: Kurt and I were lying in a matchbox. Georg was standing at the foot of the box, saying: You have it made. He slid the cover shut, up to our necks. In the dream the tree on the cover of the matchbox was a beech. It rustled. Georg said: You sleep, I'll look after the forest. Then it will be your turn. At the foot of the matchbox a fire was burning.

Kurt hadn't shown up for work since Georg's death. Instead of going to the slaughterhouse, he rode into town.

The girl next door with the speckled eyes came through the garden late one evening and knocked on Kurt's door. Are you ill? she asked, you're not in bed.

Kurt said: As you can see, I'm standing in the door-way.

The dogs were barking in the yard, because the wind was beating against the gutters. The girl from next door had switched off the light in her house. Her window was dark. She was dressed too lightly and had wrapped her arms around herself. She was wearing embroidered summer slippers with cork heels. Because of her thick woollen socks, the slippers were too small; her heels were sticking out.

She wanted Kurt to give her Georg's address in Germany. She tried to stand still but she shivered and wobbled. The light fell on her slippers. In the darkness, her legs stuck out of her socks as thin as a white goat's. She wasn't wearing any nylons.

Kurt asked: What do you want his address for? He didn't even say goodbye to you.

She lowered her head: We didn't quarrel, and I need medicine.

Then go to a doctor, said Kurt.

Tereza got a blank medical certificate for Kurt to fill out so that he wouldn't lose his job. The certificate cost a carton of Marlboros. When Kurt offered to pay her, Tereza said: I stole them out of my father's wardrobe.

In Mother's letter, behind the back-pains, I read: I got the big forms. The policeman filled them in for me and Grandmother. He said that you have to fill yours in yourself, your Romanian is good enough. I told him you probably didn't even want to go with us. Then everything will take longer, in his opinion. Toni the clockmaker thinks you'll reconsider. He would happily go with us in your place, but how?

I explained everything to Grandmother, she had to sign too. You can't read the signature, but it's her writing. It would be worse if you could read it, because she's forgotten

227

her name. She sang a little bit. I'm glad I don't know what's going through her head when she stares at me like a polecat.

Today I sold off the furniture in the front room. No one wanted the rug, it's all motheaten. I'm enclosing money for two months' rent. After that you'll have to fend for yourself. I don't want you to stay here. You've still got your life ahead of you.

I filled in the blanks on the form: Birth, School, Work, Father's military history. I could hear his songs for the Führer. I could see his hoe in the garden and his damn stupid plants. I didn't know whether they had milk thistles in Germany, they certainly had plenty of former SS-men, back from the war.

Grandfather, the barber, Toni the clockmaker, Father, the priest, and the schoolteacher all referred to Germany as the Motherland. Even though it was fathers who had marched off into the world for Germany, still it was the Motherland.

By leaving, Georg had beaten a path for Edgar and me to follow. Out of the cul-de-sac, he used to say. And six weeks later he was lying on the pavement in the Frankfurt winter.

The butcher birds stayed in Kurt's wardrobe, in a shoe. In their place, Georg had flown out of his cul-de-sac into the sack with the window. Maybe the puddle where his head rested reflected the sky. Everyone had a friend in every wisp of cloud . . . nevertheless Edgar and I followed Georg. Edgar too filled in his application to emigrate. In his jacket pocket was the telegram announcing Georg's death.

Kurt didn't feel up to emigrating. There's no sense in staying here, he said, but you two go on ahead. I'll follow. He rocked on his chair, the floorboards creaked to the rhythm of despair. But despair wasn't enough to frighten us.

I'm an accomplice of the blood-guzzlers, said Kurt, that's why I don't get fired. Once you leave, I'll be all theirs. Since the summer, the prisoners have been bussed out onto the fields behind the slaughterhouse. They're digging a sewer. If they get tired, they're set upon by dogs. They're carried back to the bus and lie there until it drives back to town at six o'clock. I photograph them from my office. Two blood-guzzlers caught me by surprise, said Kurt, they were the first to know. Maybe the others all know about it by now. I keep the films in the back of the wardrobe. That's how I found Georg's poems, too. I'll take them to Tereza and pick them up before I go see Edgar's father. He's supposed to send them to you by way of the customs official.

Maybe I will lose my job after all, said Kurt. Send me two pictures when you're in Germany, one of the window and one of the pavement. They'll reach me, Pjele knows how much they'll hurt.

Tereza cried when she heard that I'd filled out the forms. Her boyfriend had left her. He had said: A woman without children is like a tree without fruit. He and Tereza had gone to the tram stop together. He had pointed to each person in line and told her what illness each had.

Tereza said: You don't even know them. But he diagnosed away: He's got it in the liver, and she's got it in the lung. When he couldn't think of anything else he said: Look at the way he's holding his head. She has a bad heart. And his larynx is shot. Tereza asked: What about me? He didn't answer. Emotions, he said, have nothing to do with the head, they're all in the glands.

The nut in Tereza's armpit had recently started to hurt. It stretched across a vein that ran from her armpit to her breast.

I didn't want Tereza to be alone, and I said: Hold on to Kurt. Tereza nodded. You're taking part of me away, she said, and you're giving the rest to Kurt. And besides, I'm only half the nut anyway. It's easy to share out something that isn't whole anymore.

Now it was my turn at the handle in the birch trunk. Tereza knew that the door would close between us, that I wouldn't be allowed back into the country to visit her.

I know we're never going to see each other again, she said.

I had told Kurt as well: Hold on to Tereza. A friendship isn't like a jacket that you can pass on to me, he said. I could slip it on. It might even look as though it fitted, from the outside, but on the inside it wouldn't keep me warm.

Whatever we said became final. The words in our mouths do as much damage as our feet on the grass—every goodbye was like that.

Who loves and leaves turned out to be us. We had come under the curse of the song:

God shall punish him
with the pinching beetle
the howling wind
the dust of the earth.

Mother came into town on the early train. She took a tranquilizer on the train and went from the station to the hairdresser's. It was the first time in her life she had been to a hairdresser. She was having her braid cut off before emigrating.

But why, your braid is a part of you, I said.

That may be, but it's no part of Germany.

Who says?

You have a hard time if you arrive in Germany with a braid, she said. I'm going to cut off Grandmother's myself. The old barber is dead, and a hairdresser in the city would have no patience with her because she won't sit still in front of the mirror. I'll have to tie her to a chair.

My heart was racing, she said. The old man who cut off my braid had a light hand. The young man who washed my hair afterward had a heavy hand. I flinched when the scissors came near me. It was like being at the doctor's.

Mother now had a perm. In spite of the cold, she didn't

tie her headscarf on, in order to show off her new curls. She carried her hacked-off braid in a plastic bag.

Will you take it with you? I asked.

She shrugged her shoulders.

We went into one shop after another. She bought her trousseau for Germany: A new rolling pin and pastry board, a nut grinder, complete services for meals, for wine, for dessert. And a new set of stainless cutlery. New underwear for herself and Grandmother.

Fit for a bride, she said, and glanced at her dead watch. You can send a crate weighing up to a hundred and twenty kilos to Germany on the train. The old wristwatch on her arm had a new band. What time is it? asked Mother.

My singing grandmother didn't have to have her braid cut off. When Mother returned from the city, she was lying dead on the floor with a piece of apple in her mouth. Death had deprived her of her share of the trousseau. The bite of apple was stuck between her lips. She hadn't choked on it. The peel was red.

The next day, the policeman couldn't find an apple that had been bitten into anywhere in the house.

Maybe she ate up the apple and saved the first bite for last, said Toni the clockmaker.

She has to be taken off the forms, said the policeman. Mother gave him money.

She's been running around in the world for such a long time, said Mother, she really might have waited until we got to Germany. They have coffins there too. But she can't stand me, that's why she's shut her eyes now. That's what she must have been scheming when she used to stare at me like a polecat. Now I have to see about the gravediggers and the priest. She'll have to be buried here. That's the way she wanted it, for me to just drop everything for her.

Rigor mortis had set in. Mother and Toni the clockmaker cut off the dead woman's clothes with scissors and stripped her to the skin. Mother fetched a bowl of water and a white cloth. Toni the clockmaker said: Laying out a corpse isn't something kin should do. A stranger has to do it, otherwise everybody will die. He washed Grandmother's face, neck, hands, and feet. Only yesterday she walked past my window, he said. Who would have guessed that I'd be washing her today? I'm not embarrassed that she's naked. He cut open a pair of the new underwear with the scissors. Mother sewed them back together on the dead woman.

Cleanliness is next to godliness, I thought, she won't go to Heaven dirty. There's no other way, said Toni the clockmaker, her body won't help anymore, it's not possible to bend her anymore. And to me he said: You could give us a hand, you know.

I took some thread out of the sewing box and threaded a thicker needle, doubling the thread. I laid the needle on a chair. Leave the thread single, said Mother, it's strong enough. It'll hold till she gets to Heaven. She made big stitches and thick knots at the ends. She had mislaid her scissors and bit the ends of thread off the dead woman with her teeth.

Grandmother's mouth was open, although she had a cloth tied around her chin. Rest your heart-beast, I said to her.

Mother lived in Augsburg. She sent a letter with her back-pains to Berlin. She wasn't quite sure it was really her, and so the sender's name she wrote on the envelope was that of the widow she was renting a room from: Helene Schall.

Mother wrote: Frau Schall was once a refugee herself. There she was after the war with three children to look after and no husband. She got her children through all by herself, and now she's sitting pretty. As a widow here you can live well enough on a state pension. Well, I'm happy for her.

Frau Schall says that Landshut is much smaller than Augsburg. But how can that be, so many people from our village live there? Frau Schall showed me the map. But there are more names on that map than dresses in the shop windows here, and who can afford them anyway?

When I read what it says on the buses in town, I feel a tugging at the back of my head. I read the street names out loud. By the time the bus has passed, I've forgotten them all again. I keep the picture of our home in the drawer of my bedside table, so that I don't bump into it during the day. But at night, before I switch off the light, I look at it. Then I have to bite my lips, and I'm glad that it will soon be dark in the room.

They have good streets here, but everything's so spread

out. I'm not used to asphalt, it makes my feet hurt, and my brain. I get as tired here in a day as I do back home in a year.

That's not home, other people live there now, I wrote to Mother. Home is where you are now.

On the envelope I wrote in big letters: Frau Helene Schall. I wrote Mother's name in parentheses underneath, much smaller. I imagined Mother between parentheses— walking, eating, sleeping, loving me in fear—just like the ones on the envelope. Floor, table, chair, and bed all belonged to Frau Schall.

And Mother wrote back to me: How would you know where home is? The place where Toni the clockmaker tends the graves, that's home.

Edgar lived in Cologne. The two of us received identical letters, with crossed axes on them: You have been sentenced to death, we'll get you soon.

They were postmarked Vienna.

Edgar and I talked on the telephone, we didn't have enough money to visit each other. We didn't have enough voice for the telephone, either. We weren't in the habit of giving out secrets over the phone, our tongues were tied by fear.

The death threats came to me by telephone as well, in German, through the same receiver I had to hold against my cheek when I talked to Edgar. While I spoke, I felt as if we'd brought Captain Pjele along with us.

Edgar was still living in the transit hostel. An old fart in the prime of life, he joked, a washed-up schoolteacher. Like me two months earlier, he now had to prove that he'd been fired in Romania for political reasons.

Witnesses aren't enough, said the official. Only a document with an official stamp on it will do.

Where from?

The official shrugged his shoulders and balanced his ballpoint pen against a vase. The pen promptly fell over.

Because of how we'd been fired, we didn't get any unemployment benefits. We had to be careful with our money and couldn't see each other as often as we would have liked.

We went to Frankfurt twice to see the place where Georg had died. The first time we couldn't take any photographs for Kurt. The second time we were tough enough to click away. But by then Kurt was already lying in the graveyard.

We looked at the window from inside and out, at the pavement from above and below. Down the long corridor of the transit hostel, a child ran, panting. We walked on tiptoe. Edgar took the camera out of my hand and said: We'll come back, the pictures won't come out if you're crying.

．　．　．

At the cemetery, we walked down the central path. The stillness of the ivy made me want to tear it down. On one grave stood a sign:

This gravesite is in a neglected condition. We ask that this gravesite be tidied up within a month. Otherwise it will be leveled. The Graveyard Administration.

At Georg's grave I had no tears. Edgar stuck the tips of his shoes into the wet soil at the grave's edge. He said: He's down there. He took a clod of earth and threw it up in the air. We heard it fall. He took another and dropped it in his jacket pocket. We didn't hear that one. Edgar looked at his palms. What a mess, he said. I knew he didn't just mean the dirt. The grave lay there like a sack. And the window, I thought to myself, has to be just the illusion of a window. I had touched it, and it felt quite ordinary to my hands; to open and shut the window was no harder than to open and shut my eyes. The real window had to be down there in the grave.

Whatever has taken a life will be swept away, I thought to myself. I couldn't picture a coffin, only a window.

I didn't know how the word transfinite came to be here in the graveyard. But beside this grave, I realized what it must always have meant.

I never forgot again.

I could have said to Tereza: Transfinite is a window that doesn't disappear once someone has fallen from it. I didn't want to write that in a letter. It was no concern of Captain

Pjele's what transfinite meant. He was too vile to think of that word in connection with himself. He made graveyards even in places where he had never set foot. He probably knew quite a few windows on quite a few corridors.

When Edgar and I left the graveyard, the trees were blowing. The sky pressed down on their crooked branches. Frozen tulips and freesias stood on the graves as if on tables. Edgar cleaned the soles of his shoes with a little stick. The tree trunks had to have had door handles in them. Blind as I was, I didn't see them. Just as back then, in the woods.

Behind Mother's back-pains I read: This week my crateful of things from Romania arrived. The rolling pin and the pastry board are missing. On Saturday afternoon I brought a couple of pigeons home in my coat pockets. They'll make good soup, I thought. Frau Schall said that's not allowed, the pigeons belong to the city. She made me take the pigeons back. I assured her that no one had seen me. The pigeons could have flown away, I said. If pigeons let themselves get caught, they have only themselves to blame, even if they belong to the city. There are more than enough in the park anyway.

I had to stick the pigeons back in my coat and take them out of the house. I wanted to let them go a couple of streets away. If they belong to the city, I thought to myself, let them find their own way back. There was no one on the street just then. I put them down in the grass by the side of the road. And do you suppose they flew away? I flapped my hands at them, but they didn't budge. Then a child came along on a bicycle, and got off. He asked what was going on. These two pigeons, I said, they won't be on their way. The child said: Then let them stay put, what's it to you? When the boy had ridden off, a man came along and said: Those pigeons are from the park, how did they get here? I said: The boy with the bicycle left them. He yelled at me: What do you mean, that's my grandson. I didn't know that, I said. And I really hadn't. Then I had to stick the pigeons in my coat pockets again. Because of the way the man looked at me, I said: Everybody just stands there, nobody wants to go to any trouble. I'm taking these pigeons back to the park myself right this minute.

Kurt sent a long letter, via the customs official, containing a list of people killed while attempting to flee, the butcher bird poems, and photographs of blood-guzzlers and prisoners. One of the photographs was of Captain Pjele.

Tereza died, it said in the letter. When she touched her leg with her finger, it left a dent in the skin. Her legs were like hoses, the pills couldn't get rid of the water anymore, it climbed up to her heart. In the last weeks, Tereza got radiation; she became feverish and puked.

I stood by her until the time she visited you. It was Pjele who sent her. I didn't want her to go. She said: You're just envious, that's all.

After she came back from Germany, she avoided me. She went and reported back. I only saw her again twice and asked for the return of everything that she had been keeping. She gave it all back to me. But it still wouldn't surprise me if Pjele took it all out of his desk one day.

I've applied to emigrate, we'll see each other in the spring.

Tereza's death hurt me so much, it was as if I had two heads smashing into each other. One was full of mown love, the other of hate. I wanted the love to grow back. It grew like grass and straw, all mixed up together, and turned into an icy affirmation on my brow. That was my damn stupid plant.

But three weeks before the long letter, Edgar and I received two identical telegrams:

Kurt was found dead in his apartment. He hanged himself with a rope.

Who had sent the telegrams? I read out loud, as if I were singing for Captain Pjele. My tongue shot up through my brow while I sang, as though the tip of it were tied fast to a baton wielded by Captain Pjele.

Edgar came to see me. We compared our two telegrams. Edgar tilted the chicken-torture, the ball swung, the beaks

240

pecked on the board. I watched the chickens calmly. I wasn't envious or selfish. Just afraid. So afraid I didn't want to grab the chicken-torture out of Edgar's hand.

It's no accident that mail travels in sacks, I said. Sacks full of mail take longer on the road than sacks full of life. The white chicken, the red, the black, I wanted to look at each one in turn. But their order was all mixed up because of their frantic pecking. Not the sacks, though; they were in order: the belt, the window, the nut, and the rope.

You and your Swabian sacks, said Edgar. Anyone who hears that is bound to think you've lost your mind.

We laid Kurt's photographs out on the floor. We sat over them just as we had done once before in the boxwood garden. I had to glance up quickly at the ceiling to check that its white was not the white of the sky.

The last photograph showed Captain Pjele crossing Trajan Square. In one hand he carried a package wrapped in white paper. With the other he was leading a child.

On the back of the photograph Kurt had written:
Grandfather buying cake.

I wished that Captain Pjele would carry a sack with all his dead. I wished his hacked-off hair would smell like a newly mown graveyard whenever he sat at the barber's. I wished his crimes would reek when he sat down at the table with his grandson after work. That the boy would be disgusted by the fingers that were feeding him cake.

I felt my mouth opening and closing:
Kurt said once, these children are already accomplices.

When their fathers kiss them goodnight, they smell that they've been drinking blood in the slaughterhouse, and they want to go there too.

Edgar moved his head as if to put in a word, but he was silent.

We were sitting and staring at the pictures on the floor. I picked up the picture of the grandfather. I took a close look at the child. Then at the grandfather's white package.

We still say: My barber and my nail-clippers, while there are others who won't ever lose another button.

My legs had fallen asleep from sitting.

When we don't speak, said Edgar, we become unbearable, and when we do, we make fools of ourselves.